HONEYSUCKLE ROSE

Buck and his band are high-tailing across Texas in one real mean band bus, following those Tequila Sunrises, leaving behind them enough empty six-packs to recycle into a medium-sized bomber.

Buck is a man who turns his regrets into song, his love into music. And when he takes up with beautiful Lily, Buck's song is only for her.

Warner Bros.
A Warner Communications Company
presents

A Sydney Pollack/Gene Taft Production
A Film by Jerry Schatzberg

Willie Nelson   Dyan Cannon
Amy Irving

Honeysuckle Rose

also starring
Slim Pickens

Executive Producer
Sydney Pollack

Screenplay by Carol Sobieski and
William D. Wittliff and John Binder

Based on the Story by
Gosta Steven and Gustav Molander

Produced by
Gene Taft

Directed by
Jerry Schatzberg

Original Songs Composed by Willie Nelson.
Performed by Willie Nelson and Family

HONEYSUCKLE ROSE

Robert Alley

Screenplay by Carol Sobieski and
William D. Wittliff and John Binder

Based on the Story by Gosta Steven and
Gustav Molander

BANTAM BOOKS
TORONTO · NEW YORK · LONDON

HONEYSUCKLE ROSE
A Bantam Book / August 1980

ACKNOWLEDGMENTS

Grateful acknowledgment is made for permission to reprint the following copyright material:

SAD SONGS AND WALTZES, *words and music by Willie Nelson. Copyright © 1964 by Tree Publishing Co., Inc.*

HEAVEN AND HELL, *words and music by Willie Nelson. Copyright © 1974 by Willie Nelson Music, Inc.*

CRAZY, *words and music by Willie Nelson. Copyright © 1961 by Tree Publishing Co., Inc.*

IF YOU WANT ME TO LOVE YOU I WILL, *words and music by Willie Nelson. Copyright © 1980 by Willie Nelson Music, Inc.*

FUNNY HOW TIME SLIPS AWAY, *words and music by Willie Nelson. Copyright © 1961 by Tree Publishing Co., Inc.*

ON THE ROAD AGAIN, *words and music by Willie Nelson. Copyright © 1980 by Willie Nelson Music, Inc.*

WHISKEY RIVER, *words and music by Willie Nelson. Copyright © 1976 by Willie Nelson Music, Inc.*

GOOD HEARTED WOMAN, *words and music by Willie Nelson. Copyright © 1971 by Willie Nelson Music, Inc.*

YESTERDAY'S WINE, *words and music by Willie Nelson. Copyright © 1971 by Willie Nelson Music, Inc.*

YOU SHOW ME YOURS AND I'LL SHOW YOU MINE, *words and music by Kris Kristofferson. Copyright © 1976 by Resaca Music Publishing Company.*

LOVING HER IS EASIER THAN ANYTHING I'LL EVER DO AGAIN, *words and music by Kris Kristofferson © 1970 by Combine Music Corp.*

TILL I GAIN CONTROL, *words and music by Rodney Crowell. Copyright © 1976 by Tessa Publishing Company.*

ISBN 0-553-14332-8

Published simultaneously in the United States and Canada

Bantam Books are published by Bantam Books, Inc. Its trademark, consisting of the words "Bantam Books" and the portrayal of a bantam, is Registered in U.S. Patent and Trademark Office and in other countries. Marca Registrada. Bantam Books, Inc., 666 Fifth Avenue, New York, New York 10103.

PRINTED IN THE UNITED STATES OF AMERICA

0 9 8 7 6 5 4 3 2 1

HONEYSUCKLE ROSE

1

Morning comes quickly to south Texas. A thin lavender line appears on the horizon between the inky earth and the star-riddled sky, like the glow of a distant city or one of those sprawling truck stops that service the semis traveling between Laredo and San Antonio. But usually there's no city and no resting place, just rolling sandy hills covered with mesquite and hackberry trees, and a little grass in the gullies where the moisture collects, all of it appearing in a pale wash of light. Telephone poles stand in drunken formation along the side of the road, and dust rises up behind the bus and hangs there in a haze. Strands of barbed wire strung on endless, twisted fenceposts hold clumps of tumbleweed blown all the way up out of Mexico or the dried corpses of coyotes crucified by the ranchers to keep the live ones at bay. Sometimes a house takes shape in the distance, a square of unnatural brilliance glowing from the kitchen window. Swaybacked cattle huddle next to the water tank, while an old yellow sheepdog howls soundlessly at the intruder.

There was no sign of people that July morning, just the awesome, endless country, the rattle of the old six-cylinder engine, and, for Buck Bonham, the memory of last night's music and the feel of the wheel in his hands. Buck had been on the road for twenty years, and yet morning could still surprise him. He was a night critter, he loved the sounds in the auditoriums and dance halls where his band played, the smell of good weed and the touch of strange hands, and the aimless talk as the band drove on through the darkness toward the next stand. But he also loved the dawn. For him it was the end of a good day and the beginning of another. He was alone then, surrounded by exhausted companions, the taste of Pearl beer in his mouth, and, if he was lucky, the makings of a new song in his mind.

The words came on him like the light, suddenly and mysteriously, without any source he could identify. As always, he treated them like a gift. The music was there, too, unwritten, unsung, but a powerful force that lifted the new-born lyrics.

He could never describe to someone who had not been there just what it was like to create a song at sunup, polish it at dusk, and sing it at night to an audience that thundered back its approval. No one who had been there was likely ever to forget.

He pulled the bus over onto the shoulder of the road and hauled on the emergency brake. The old springs groaned, and the sleepers in the seats behind him complained without waking. In the mirror Buck could see the disarray of all their lives, the boxes, bags, and instrument cases jammed into the overhead luggage racks, cases of empty beer bottles, blouses belonging to Bonnie, the piano player and the only woman in the group, hung on guitar string stretched between the windows. Cowboy boots lay in various attitudes along the floorboards. Their rolling hotel had once been a school bus. Half the seats had been removed and others shoved side-by-side for better sleeping and more comfortable sex, when the occasion arose. There

2

was a poker table screwed to the floor, an old refrigerator and a big tape deck hooked up to the double-barreled speakers mounted on top of the bus so they could ride into town to the sound of their own picking and singing. High, wide, and handsome. The bus was a joke all over the country music circuit, but Buck and the boys liked it. It was comfortable, with windows you could open up to the Texas air, and a hundred thousand miles of shared experience.

Most musicians would have written down the lines of the new song, but that wasn't Buck's way. Ordinarily he would have gone to the back of the bus, crawled into his seat, and slept for a few hours. Garland Ramsey could take over the driving. He was riding shotgun, his hands folded on his gut and his breath whistling through slack lips. Garland at sixty years old was the grand old man of the pickers, known from El Paso to Texarkana, and beyond. He was also Buck's best friend, although he had a good fifteen years on Buck and sometimes preached at him. Ramsey had taught him much of what he knew about the practical side of music making. They had spent endless hours chewing over every subject known to man, while one of them pushed the old bus over the back country roads. Volcanoes, astrology, seashells, and the best mescal cactus for making tequila were all subjects Ramsey had mastered, as well as the inner workings of pickup trucks, the proper use of a fence stretcher, and everything there was to know about guitars. Ramsey wasn't just a friend—he was plain good company.

Buck eased past him, swung open the door, and stepped out into the early morning. The sound of last night's music faded now as he heard the doves calling back and forth. They sat in pairs on the telephone lines, necks craned to watch this strange apparition in a battered cowboy hat. Buck bowed to them with more ceremony than he would ever have used on a live audience, and a few of them took off in an explosion of soft, downy wings, but more of them stayed behind to see him pull off his boots and then his Levis and stand there in his undershorts and T-shirt.

Leisurely Buck relieved himself against the bald front tire. Then he reached into the bus, under the seat that supported Ramsey's snoring bulk, and pulled out a pair of jogging pants and some sneakers that had once been white. He put them on, humming a little to himself, wishing he had company for the run but knowing better than to wake the others. Physical exercise was not high on their lists, unless it was dancing, roping, or shit kicking, and even that not at dawn.

He slipped expertly between the strands of barbed wire and began to jog into the red, rising Texas sun. The air was cool and sweet smelling, but in an hour it would dry out what was left of the dew and warm up the bus like an old sardine can left in the oven. That would get the boys moving, all right. Buck scattered a bunch of cows that turned in unison to stare at him with the same doleful disbelief employed by the doves. Everybody and everything in Texas knew instinctively that cowboys never walked when they didn't have to, and they sure as hell didn't *run*.

Soon he was sweating. His pigtails bobbed and slapped him in the face, so he tied them up behind his head with the red bandanna. Buck didn't want to be distracted—he had his song to think about and side-winder rattlers and gopher holes to watch out for. Pigtails weren't exactly pretty on a man his age—on a man any age, for that matter—but he felt comfortable with them. His wife Viv had braided his hair one night before a concert, as a joke. He discovered that the pigtails kept his hair out of his eyes while he performed, and he had decided to keep them. Ramsey had had some trouble accepting the new style, but the younger musicians had taken it in stride. Those pigtails had earned Buck a lot of press in the beginning, and not a few fist fights in the state's less tolerant backwaters, before they became part of his trademark. If a drunk got too personal about them, Buck would be all over him like a dirty shirt. A big man could whip him, but it usually took half an hour, and by then both of them would be bleeding.

He turned around and ran back toward the bus. He could make out the words in the distance: Buck Bonham's Band, and the big white Lone Star painted on the side, covered with dust. That star was part of his trademark, too, though it had nothing to do with badges or the Texas Rangers or any of the other stock associations. Buck and his buddies were all outlaws in the country music business. They played their own way and lived their own lives, and people of all ages were drawn to their sound and their light. That's what the star on the side of the bus was all about. Buck had never taken the time to explain it. He figured that those who ought to know would know.

Heaven ain't walking on a street paved with gold,
And hell ain't a mountain of fire.

His head feeling good about the way the song was coming and his body feeling satisfied with the run, Buck headed back toward the bus. A figure appeared in the doorway and stepped down into the dust. It was Rooster. He grinned broadly, tucking his shirttails into the top of his jeans, his eyes puffy with sleep. Rooster had grown up in Mexico without Coca-Cola and Hershey bars, and he had

5

the best set of teeth in the group. He handled the electronic gear and looked after all the odds and ends, like spare parts for the bus and beer for the boys, and was as essential to the band as the harmonica player, as Ramsey or Buck himself. At least Buck made him feel that way.

"Mornin', Buck."

"Mornin', Rooster."

"We gonna hit some?"

"Sure thing."

Rooster turned to relieve himself against the front tire. Buck climbed the ladder to the top of the bus and began to root around underneath the tarpaulin. He could feel the sun on his back now, and the earth expanding, waking. Soon Buck would be asleep, leaving someone else to handle the wheel, but first they had to hit a few golf balls. Buck's interest in the game was limited to the good feel of the club smacking the ball and the satisfaction of seeing that little white point sail away into the blue sky in a perfect arch. He didn't care much about scores and handicaps, he played the game as an adventure, a kind of roundup where you beat the balls out of the weeds or the chaparral, depending on where you were, out from under cactus or creosote bush or cotton rows, just to keep it moving. Rooster took his golf seriously, however. He wanted to be the first Mexican to ever win the open at Palm Springs, and Buck was helping him.

He located the golf bag and carried it down. Rooster took the 1-wood, and Buck took the 2-wood and a handful of balls, and they stepped through the barbed wire.

"Remember," Buck said, "keep your head down."

Rooster nodded solemnly. Buck and the cows watched him trudge off, the club over one shoulder, his boots leaving splay-footed prints in the dirt. He paused at the top of the rise and flailed away at something on the ground with the club, probably a snake, a Gila monster, or a scorpion. Then he walked on, disappearing from sight.

Buck dropped the balls onto the ground. He teed one up and stood with his feet spread wide, carefully placing his hands on the club. Years of fretting and picking the guitar had left calluses on both hands that messed up his grip; he had to make adjustments. He addressed the ball and shuffled his feet. But the song wasn't done yet, the music wasn't through with him.

> Heaven is lying in my sweet baby's arms,
> And hell is when baby's not there.

Buck thought of his wife waking up in her bed, hundreds of miles from where he stood. He thought of his son, of their little spread outside of Austin, and he felt the loneliness peculiar to the road that can't be eradicated by friends or even by the cries of the crowd and the thrill of performing. Buck had never completely gotten over that loneliness, but he had learned to live with it, and he raised the club and brought it around in a clean, hard swing.

Sid woke up with a start. Dazzled by the sun, he closed his eyes again as quickly as he had opened them. He thought he had heard a distant gunshot, and he lay for a moment with his arm across his face, trying to get his bearings. The bus was not moving—not a good sign—and Buck was gone. Not a good sign, either. He wondered vaguely if they had come under attack from some crazy bastard lying in the sage with a .22-caliber rifle, and if Buck had gone after him. Sid didn't feel up to being ambushed. He had drunk too many tequila Sunrises the night before, and each tooth felt as if it wore a tiny sweater.

He sneaked a glance at his watch. It was 7:10, which meant they were hours away from where they had to be. Sid was the business manager, and it was his responsibility to get the band members to their appointments on time. He also had to collect the money and dole it out, make the deals, keep an eye on the bills for motels, food, and booze, stroke the media, and alibi for the musicians when wives and girlfriends started calling long-distance, wanting to know why their men couldn't come home, or at least to the telephone. It was no easy job. The boys complained when he pushed them too hard.

He heard the sound again, a sharp reverberating *crack*, and he turned in the seat and peered out across the scrub pasture. There was Buck, wearing his battered cowboy hat and a jogging outfit, about to drive another golf ball into the rising sun. Sid wondered what Buck's fans would think if they knew he was a golfer. Golf wasn't the most natural pastime for an outlaw picker and a traveling man who wrote songs about dying, cowpokes, unhappy love, and all the attractions of an unconventional life. Of course Buck played golf the way he did everything else, including picking and singing, with a wild individuality that turned it into something new and funky. Chances were Buck's admirers would love to watch him play golf. There wasn't much he did they didn't approve of.

Sid pulled himself erect and stepped over the boots and the beer cans left in the aisle. Everybody else was asleep, and the inside of the bus had the look of a hotel suite after an all-night orgy. He sometimes asked himself why he lived in the middle of such a mess, why he put up with the long hours and all the hassles of managing a country group, even if it was one of the best? The answer was he would rather do that than anything else.

He had to squeeze by Garland, and as he did he woke up the older man. Garland's big, doelike eyes opened, and he stared at Sid as if he had been insulted and planned to do something about it.

"Mornin', Garland."

"Sid." He blinked, then added, "What the hell time is it? Where are we?"

"Early and nowhere, looks like."

Sid stepped outside and took a deep breath of morning air. He unzipped his jeans and relieved himself against the front tire of the bus, and then slipped through the barbed-wire fence.

"Hey, Buck!"

The group's leader didn't respond, as Sid suspected he wouldn't. Sid circled around, waving his arms at the cows brought in close by their curiosity, until he could see Buck's face. Buck had leathery skin and high cheekbones, and he could have passed for a Cherokee or Comanche, except for the beard. Buck was lean as a hoe handle and just as hard. A gold stud in his left ear lobe glinted in the sun, and his expression looked peaceful, if a little sad.

"Buck," Sid hollered, "we better move it. Three hundred miles to do, and a radio interview at two o'clock."

Buck remained silent. He lined the head of the club up with another ball, drew back, and drove the ball over the rise. Admiringly, Sid watched it disappear. He wouldn't mind hitting a few himself, but they had a ways to go and people to see. It was his responsibility.

"Buck, come on."

"Heads up," Buck said.

Sid looked in time to see the ball sailing back toward him. He jumped to one side as it whistled past and landed in the dust, rolling under the barbed wire. Buck laughed at him.

"What a great invention," Sid said. "Boomerang golf balls. How'd you do that?"

"Rooster's over there trying to hit 'em back. Watch it!"

Another ball sailed toward them. This one fell short, kicking up a puff of dust two feet from the nose of a grazing cow. Rooster appeared at the top of the rise. He took aim on the last ball and drew back the club with professional care, but after he started the swing, he looked up. He topped the ball, and it rolled away from him.

Sid and Buck both hooted.

"How many times I gotta tell you?" Buck shouted. "Keep your head down!"

The next time Rooster did as he was told, and he got a piece of the ball. It soared in the morning light, bounced, and grazed the flank of an old Hereford. The stock went galloping off.

"Come on, Rooster," Buck said. "We'll come back and kill the rest of these cows later."

2

Garland was racing the train. It was a losing proposition any way you looked at it, even though they had a head start and ten straight miles of Interstate. The bus shook with the engine's exertions, the windows rattled and wind whipped back and forth across the aisle like a tornado. The boys leaned out over one side, whistling and hog calling, while music blared from the P. A. system mounted on top. Kelly turned the volume up so high that Buck was afraid the speakers would blow. From where he sat he could see Garland hunched over the wheel, his hat pulled down around his ears, his face thrust close to the windshield as if that would make the bus roll a little faster.

Slowly the train pulled away. The engineer raised an arm to salute them, and the boys all cheered. They were awake now, ready for coffee, grits and eggs, or chicken-fried steaks, and another stand in another town. All Buck wanted was sleep. Bonnie smiled sympathetically at him from across the bus, her feet tucked under her, and the needlepoint spread on her lap. He respected her because she could live among men without ties and keep her dignity and her natural affection. She wasn't beautiful, but she wasn't ugly, either. She had blond curls, and the broad, friendly face of a sod-buster's daughter, and anybody on the bus

11

would have done anything for her, though Bonnie seldom asked for favors. She could play the piano to hell and back and drink with the best of them when she felt like it. She never judged the others, and she never messed with them, for she'd had two bad husbands, and that was enough men to last her. Still, Bonnie was family.

Buck felt equal affection for the other musicians, for Tex and his inscribed drumsticks, for Jonas on backup guitar, for big Bliss and Bo on the basses, even for red-headed Kelly and his squealing harmonica. He watched them shut their windows and gather around the table, ready for poker before breakfast, hats on at funny angles, joking and laughing. Already a joint was passing among them, the sweetish marijuana smoke mixing with the dust and the hot smell of a Texas highway in July. They would probably all be dead or burned out before they were his age, but that was their business.

Only Garland was truly special, unique. He was not just a friend; he brought tradition, as well as his own talent, to the group, and Buck couldn't imagine playing or traveling without him.

Buck went over the words of the new song in his mind one more time. Then he closed his eyes and let the wind and the sound of the music rush over him.

Applause drowned out the last chords, the whistles and the cheers lingering in the dark hall. Buck draped an arm over the neck of his guitar and squinted at the audience. An ocean of faces stretched away, the bright coals of cigarettes like the stars' reflections. He could see girls mounted on their boyfriends' shoulders, clinging to the railing of the balcony, perched on the edge of the stage itself. Smoke drifted across the high banks of lights like hot fog, sweet smelling and intoxicating. It was a good crowd, full of heart, and hungry for the sound.

He turned toward the band, backed by a huge flag of Texas suspended from the ceiling. They were waiting for his lead. He paused and hit the strings, singing directly into the mike.

Instantly the audience recognized a new song. There was a surge of voices and applause, followed by calm as Buck and his group waded into the words they had sung together only once, just before the concert.

Buck waltzed forward during the refrain, and the girls on the edge of the stage plucked at his Levis and the boys hog-called to him. More girls stood in the wings, all pretty as they could be, shoe-horned into their jeans, their feathery hair blown dry and their nipples visible through the thin material of their blouses. They grooved with the music, all smiles and soft, insistent movements of hips and shoulders. It wasn't the sex that moved him, but the good will.

As Buck played, he instinctively let his eyes roam. He didn't really care about the size of the gate—that was Sid's problem, and at that moment Sid was off in some office with the other business-men, counting money into a pile. Buck wanted to make sure that everybody was happy, that they were with him. He saw Rooster in the wings, studying a particularly fine set of breasts, oblivious even to the music. He inched forward onto the stage. His foot slipped over the edge, and Buck saw him topple into a forest of up-raised hands. People howled with laughter as Rooster, all white teeth and red cheeks, was shoved back up onto the boards. The girl with the fine breasts hadn't even noticed the near-calamity she had caused.

When the group finished the song and the applause rolled over them, whistles took up where the music trailed off. Buck felt the best high there was: the song was good, and everybody knew it. He took off his hat and sailed it out over the audience, and more cheering rose from the crowd. Tex followed Buck's example and slid one of his drumsticks across the stage, to the girl with the breasts. She stooped to pick it up, her blond hair falling over her face like blinders. Buck knew that Tex had hand-lettered the words I Love You on the stick. The girl read the words, smiled, and nodded at the drummer. That was all it took.

Buck leaned close to the mike and thanked the crowd. "I want you all to say hello to my sister, Bonnie, on the piano."

The applause never stopped. He introduced Tex, Kelly, Jonas, Bliss, and Bo. Each of them took a little bow and hit a note on the strings. They were all a little high now, tired and happy, and ready for the finale. Buck scanned the audience again, looking for a little old lady in steel-rimmed glasses. He had passed her in the corridor before the concert, hours before, where she had been piling relish and onion onto a foot-long hotdog. "I love the tears in your songs," she had told Buck, and the girl behind the counter had added, "I like the harmonica player." Both of them were out there somewhere, and Buck waved. One of the girls riding her man piggyback had come out of the fight for Buck's hat with the prize, and she waved back at him and beat the hat against the man's head as if he were a bronco. Judging from the look on his face, he didn't mind.

"Give 'em one, Garland," Buck said, having saved the best for last. "Here he is, folks—Garland Ramsey!"

The rest of the audience came to its feet. Garland grinned and launched into a song without words, his own rendition of "I'm a Rambling Man."

Garland had the best fingers in the business, and he increased the tempo slowly but steadily.

Buck stepped to the piano and took a swig from the open bottle of tequila resting there, feeling the hot trail blaze down the middle of his insides and the mellow satisfaction that it wrought. He was having one fine time.

Garland charmed the people, his old face young in the glare of the spotlight, transformed by the music. The rhinestone snaps on his cowboy shirt gleamed, and his left boot beat out the time until the polished lizard-skin toe became a blur. The audience began to clap and cheer, urging Garland to push it, and he did. He broke off suddenly to let Kelly blow some wild harmonica, dipping and slinging his red hair out of his face. Then Garland was back again. Bo and Bliss trailed in on the basses, their long Texas frames jerking like puppets on the same string. Jonas followed, head back, mouth open. Bonnie hunched her shoulders and attacked the keys.

They went directly into the new song. Feet thundered against the floor, and people screamed encouragement until Buck thought the roof would cave in.

Just before Buck pulled the plug, he looked over and saw Garland watching him.

The parking lot stood in cool darkness. The last cars spewed gravel as they pulled out into the highway, and the musicians milled around the bus with the groupies, passing the time before they hit the road. Rooster scampered about on top, tying down the luggage and the sound equipment. He would cover it with the tarp even though he didn't have to, for there was no rain within striking distance.

Buck stood off to one side, gratefully breathing

the night air. He swept the beaded headband off and shoved it down into the pocket of his jeans. He felt good, and ready for the trip: they were going home.

Sid stepped into the circle of light around the stage door.

"It was a good one, huh, Sid?"

The manager ambled over, fishing a Camel out of his shirt pocket. His suit jacket had darts sewn into the sides and wide lapels, and he wore plain black boots. It didn't take a genius to tell that Sid was no guitar picker.

"I think you're in trouble, Buck," he said.

If there was trouble around, Sid would be the first to notice. But that was part of his job. "How's that?" Buck asked.

"Hard as you've tried to avoid it all these years, I believe you're catching on."

Then Sid laughed and slapped him on the back, and Buck couldn't keep the smile off his face. It was a real compliment, coming from Sid. He knew they had done well. They had made money that night, and they had touched the people, and they would all come back to hear Buck Bonham's Band if they got the chance. That was the most important thing as far as Buck was concerned, not the money and not even the glory.

"Oh," Buck said, "maybe I can manage to screw that up, if I catch it in time. I'll work on it."

"I'm just afraid you will."

Sid wasn't joking, not entirely, and Buck knew it. He was capable of screwing things up if he felt that the members were getting stale and the music suffering. Or if an impulse led him off in another direction. Buck's unpredictability had always bothered Sid. It had taken Buck years, and a lot of Garland's help, to get where he was that night.

Buck and his band played real music: they didn't cheat, and they didn't hoke it up, and people respected that. They were all making good money now, they were known, but Buck was no more proud of himself than he had been in the beginning, when he was just starting out. He had played good music then, too, and the songs had come to him on invisible wings, just as they did now.

"You still don't get it, do you, Sid?"

Sid didn't get it. He didn't say so, but Buck could tell from the way he stood there shuffling his boots in the gravel.

"Success," Buck told him. "That's somebody else's judgment."

Sid still didn't say anything, but he stopped shuffling his feet. Buck saw Tex slip through the stage door, pulling a girl behind him.

"Failure, same thing," Buck said. "It's got nothing to do with me. That's your territory."

Sid nodded, without conviction. He assumed Buck was just shooting the bull, but he was serious.

"Hard to believe, ain't it?" Buck said.

He turned toward the band members. "Let's take it home, boys."

They all filed on board. Buck was the last one up, and he went directly to the back of the bus and took a Pearl out of the icebox. He pulled the tab and dropped it through the hole, then tipped the can back. The cold beer was his reward, and he prolonged the swallow. He was still a little high on the tequila and the crowd that night, but not too far gone to drive. He had pushed that bus over the roads when he was in much worse shape, and he had lived to tell about it.

He went back up front and settled into the worn driver's seat. He felt around on the floorboards until he found the key. He slipped it into the ignition and began to coax the motor to life. It sputtered, spat, complained, and finally caught, and the bus shuddered as if dreading the miles ahead. He released the emergency brake and opened the side vent for some good night air. He swung the door shut and jammed the lock in place. Behind him, some of the band members were already prepared for sleep, their boots up on the seat backs and their hats tipped over their eyes. Bo and Bliss had settled down for some cutthroat five-card stud, and Bonnie bent over her needlepoint. One big family, ready to roll.

Buck took another swallow of beer, then set the bus in gear. They were rolling out of the lot when he remembered Tex. He jammed on the brakes, turning to count heads. Then he leaned on the horn.

The stage door opened, and Tex ran through the light, pulling up his trousers. He boarded the bus fastening his belt buckle, ignoring the hoots and the laughter from the dark interior.

Buck pulled onto the highway. He glanced in the side mirror and saw the girl with the fine breasts standing in the stage door, buttoning her shirt with one hand and raising the other in farewell.

3

"Here you go, Buck."

Garland handed him a cold beer and slipped into the shotgun seat. Driving, drinking, and talking was a nightly ritual for them, and one Buck looked forward to. They had been on the highway for less than an hour, and already Rooster was snoring directly in back of them, resting up for his turn behind the wheel when dawn came. The yellow lines in the middle of the Interstate rose up in the headlights and slipped past the bus, broken and unchanging. They always reminded Buck of machine gun fire in a comic book; sometimes he counted them just to keep awake.

"What are we gonna talk about tonight, Garland? Volcanoes?" Garland had once told him about a volcano that started out in a perfectly flat field in Central America. At the end of the first day the hill was as big as a house. At the end of the second day it was the size of a small building, and after a week it had swelled into a mountain. The top blew off, and so much ash rained into the air that people could see the cloud hundreds of miles away. Lava poured down the mountain and into the ocean, producing so much steam that it cooked the coconuts on all the trees. At least that's what Garland claimed. "Earthquakes?" Buck prompted. "Horse trailers?"

But Garland just shrugged and stared out the window. He had something else on his mind, that much was clear. Buck remembered the look Garland had given him during the concert, sly and kind of sorrowful. Buck could sense the tension.

Garland took out his billfold. He opened it up and began to flip through his collection of photographs, all neatly contained in plastic. Buck knew he was looking at the pictures of his wife and kids, and he felt a twinge of guilt. Buck had no photographs of Viv or of his son Jamie. He missed them both, and he could clearly see their faces in his mind whenever he thought of them, which was often. But he had never managed to get the right sort of pictures taken, and those he carried with him always got creased or soaked with beer, and somehow that seemed more disloyal than carrying no pictures at all. And then Buck didn't believe in feeling sorry for himself. He loved his family, but he also loved the road; he could handle his regrets.

Garland said, without looking at him, "We done a lot of living on this road, ain't we, Buck? You and me."

"Twenty-some-odd years worth." Buck didn't keep a real close record. He looked down at Garland's right hand, lighted up in the glow from the dashboard. There were brown spots on it, like an old man gets, and the index finger looked stranger than ever. Garland had broken it rodeoing in Oklahoma City, before Buck met him. If he had messed up his left hand instead of his right, he wouldn't have been able to fret and so wouldn't have ended up playing a guitar in a roving country band. He wouldn't have taught Buck all he knew, and maybe their lives would have been different. Buck suspected they would have been on the road anyway, selling shoes or seeds or barber supplies. A country musician wasn't much different from a traveling salesman, when you got right down to it.

Garland sighed and put the wallet away. "Didn't start with nothing but a guitar and a hard-on," he said.

"Well, hell, Garland, you still got the guitar, ain't you?" Garland had stepped into that one. Buck laughed and slapped him on the knee, determined to cheer him up.

They rode on for a while. Buck thought about the early days, about the one-night stands in the honky-tonks, about the fights and the short receipts and the people whose beautiful notions and often sorrowful lives had fed the flames of his own inspiration. Once he had seen a man shot and stabbed in a bar outside San Angelo, where the band was playing. The man lay dying in a pool of blood after his attackers fled. He said he wanted to hear the song "Honeysuckle Rose" one more time, and Buck and Viv had sung it for him, their faces close together before the mike, holding each other up with their voices, their eyes locked in the knowledge that their words and their music were the last things that cowpoke would ever hear. Viv had traveled with Buck then, before their child was born.

"Time to hang it up, Buck."

"In favor of what?"

The words sounded stronger than Buck intended. He saw Garland smiling in the reflecting windshield, and Buck smiled, too. Nothing was so serious they couldn't talk about it, as he had often said. He knew now what was bothering Garland—the same thing that had bothered him off and on for years. But for some reason Buck was more reluctant to listen tonight.

"My boys grew up without me even noticing," Garland said.

Buck nodded; it was a familiar refrain.

"And Lily's home from college this summer."

The last time Buck had seen Garland's daughter, she'd had pigtails. Of course Buck now had pigtails. It was a good joke, and he wanted to share it, but he kept his mouth shut and his eyes on the road. Finally Garland asked him, "You aware that I'm quitting, Buck?"

"Quitting?"

This time Garland nodded, a slow, ponderous motion that had more conviction in it than Buck felt comfortable with. He would just have to change Garland's mind.

"Sid tells me we're about to 'go large,'" Buck said.

"You believe that?"

"Maybe." Sid was always hustling and talking grand, but it was true that their notoriety had spread all over the Southwest. Country music was big business now, and they needed fresh sounds to record and fresh faces to promote. "Hell, they've used everybody else up. They gotta get around to guys like us sooner or later."

"If that happens," Garland said, "then you're gonna tell me we're too big to quit, right?"

He *would* tell him that, as a matter of fact. Buck and Garland had done as much as anybody else, and more than most, to create the new country sound that had nothing to do with Nashville and all the worn-out tinsel in that town. Austin was their home, and the west was in their sound, and there were plenty of people all over the country now who wanted to hear it.

But Garland wasn't in a reasonable mood.

"You see the little ratchets in the road?" Buck asked.

"Ratchets?"

"In the center lines. The bumps."

Garland leaned forward and peered into the night. Then he cut his eyes at Buck, realizing that he was distracting him on purpose. "Buck, I mean it. Lily's twenty-one. I have a hard time remembering what she looks like without taking out her picture."

"I'll bet you five hundred American dollars," Buck said, "that I can thread this mother back and forth between the ratchets ten times without hitting one."

It was an interesting proposition. Garland took a long drag on his Pearl, trying to ignore it. "I'm serious," he said, meaning the quitting.

"So am I."

"Ten times in a row?" Garland asked, getting sucked in. "Or ten times between here and Austin?"

"In a row."

"Just the front wheels?"

"Front or back." Buck had him now. "Nothing hits nothing."

Garland was about to accept. Then he caught himself and said, "Buck, I'm *quitting*."

"Five hundred dollars," Buck persisted. "Are you in or out?"

Garland took another swallow of beer and braced himself in the seat.

"In the bet," he said, "and out of the band."

The bus swerved across the highway. Rooster rolled out of his bunk and hit the floor heavily, and plastic plates and cups from the overhead shelf rained down on him. Buck swerved back, just making it inside the second marker, and Bo and Bliss rolled from their bunks, on top of Rooster. He cursed in Spanish. Buck whooped in answer, cutting the wheel to the left again. Groceries slid off the shelf. Buck could hear the soup and beer cans rolling back and forth, and some good English swearing now, as well as groans, general complaints, and some laughter.

He glanced at Garland to see if he shared the mood of Buck's antics, hoping he could drive the older man out of his woeful mood with some crazy behavior. It had worked before, but this time Garland shouted, "I'm trying to give you notice—"

Buck hauled on the wheel; someone else behind him lost his grip on the seat.

"Hell, there's plenty of pickers can take my place, Buck."

Buck was counting the markers in the highway. "Who said there wasn't? Six—seven—"

"Don't make me feel bad, Buck. I know what I gotta do. It's past due."

Buck ran over the last marker. He felt a thump beneath the left front tire, and knew he had lost more than the bet. "I ain't judging you, Garland."

Buck straightened the bus up. In the mirror he could see the band members tussling in the aisle, laughing and tossing hats and boots around. Just like a bunch of kids, Buck thought. Only Bonnie seemed unperturbed. She sat braced in her seat, bent over her needlepoint, ignoring the roughhousing that always broke out toward the end of a tour. She looked up and gave Buck that wistful little smile.

Garland looked uncomfortable with his decision. He had already forgotten the bet.

"Hell," Buck said, trying to cheer him up, "it probably takes more nerve to quit than it does to keep on going. I just don't know who I'm going to talk to at night."

"I want to be with my family, Buck."

"You'll just make a nuisance of yourself around home."

"Well, maybe. But at least I want to give it a

try. We get old too soon, Buck, and smart too late."

Buck didn't have a comeback. He had always known that Garland would leave the group sooner or later, but he had always managed to think of it as later. It didn't seem like twenty years ago that they had started out on the road together. It seemed more like yesterday.

"You ought to slow down, too," Garland said. "Eleven months on the road every year—you don't need that."

Buck did need it. Garland had needed it, too, he was just forgetting. He needed the motion and the new towns, the bright lights and the air of expectancy, the fast food and the comradeship. But it was more than that, more than the strange women in the beginning and the good money now. It was the satisfaction of living day-to-day off your own talent, and it was the thrill of performing.

"What would I do at home?" Buck asked.

"We could drink a respectable amount of tequila. Play some golf. Cut a couple of records. Party. Curl up like fat cats and get old gently."

Buck laughed out loud. "Old, shit! I'm not looking to get old." He couldn't believe that Garland meant it. "Maybe you are getting soft in the head. Maybe it is better that you're quitting."

Garland didn't answer. They rode on in silence for a while, watching the tandem trucks rise up out of the hollows and pass in a blaze of lights. There were few cars on the road. The land seemed even more huge at night, the laboring old six-cylinder engine unequal to the distances. Buck didn't like the idea of driving them alone. "Damn, this is gonna feel like divorce, Garland. Let's quit talking about it."

4

Buck woke up to the sound of his own voice singing "Uncloudy Day." Rooster was driving, the music blaring from the speakers, the morning sun filling the bus with a hard, clean light. They were crossing the Balcones Fault, on the outskirts of Austin. Scrub growth cedar fled past, as did mailboxes, houses, pickups. He glimpsed a rancher standing on the side of the road, letters in his hand, his baffled face turned toward the music.

The rancher was replaced by a house up close to the road, a window full of children's faces, and a woman in an apron standing next to a washing machine on the porch. The unpainted clapboards reminded Buck of his own house. The yard was patrolled by chickens, and a bay pony crowded the fence.

Then Buck saw the plywood nailed to the gate and the message scrawled in black paint: Pony 4 Sale. He had missed Jamie's birthday the week before, and on impulse he jumped up and told Rooster to stop the bus. Rooster backed up along the highway and down the rutted road toward the ranchhouse.

An hour later the bus rolled into the city. Austin was the home of the state legislature and

the state university, but the south side where Buck
and his friends congregated resembled any Texas
cow town. The narrow streets were lined with
cafés and bars, hole-in-the-wall restaurants that
served some of the best Mexican food anywhere,
pool halls, bail bondsmen's offices, and a tractor
dealership. There was dust on the sidewalks, and
the men standing in the storefronts all wore boots
and hats with broad brims. Buck had once been
limited to playing the small cafés when he came to
Austin. Now he and the band played the clubs
further uptown, toward the new high-rise buildings, where men in coats and ties and women in
high-heel shoes joined those in western outfits to
hear the best country music. But Buck Bonham's
Band came back across the railroad tracks to do its
eating, drinking, and visiting.

The speakers announced their arrival at the
Raw Deal Café, a favorite watering hole. An old
man standing on the corner raised his rubber-
tipped cane and shouted, "Wooooah! Sing it!"
Friends and family waiting in the parking lot
rushed toward the bus. Buck had strung a blanket
across the aisle to conceal the new passenger.
Buck's sleeve was torn, his Levis were smeared
with mud, and his good boots were covered with
manure. The pony had decided it didn't want to go
to Austin in an old school bus with a star painted
on the side, and it had taken every band member to
change the pony's mind.

They all piled off, into the midst of the wel-
coming committee. Buck was the exception. He
had a few miles to go yet, out to his little ranch in
the hills, but he called and waved to his old friends
in the lot. He saw Garland and his wife come
together in a bear hug; he would have to talk to
Garland later. Kelly was surrounded by the usual
crowd of girls, looking young and shy away from

the stage lights. Tex embraced his hometown girl, Jeannie, a cute little blond, who was as innocent as Tex was shiftless. Buck heard her ask Tex, "Did you miss me?"

"I can't count the ways," Tex said, shaking his head, playing it for all it was worth. What he meant was, he couldn't count the girls he had been with since he left Austin the last time. "The road's a hard and lonely life, babe."

"Oh, Tex." Jeannie hugged him again, and he handed her a package neatly wrapped up with yellow ribbon. Everyone crowded around, though the boys all knew what the package contained. Jeannie tore off the ribbon and the paper and held up a frilly bra—white lace and red ribbons, with two holes in it. Some of the men hooted. Jeannie blushed and looked up at Tex skeptically, but he just shrugged.

Buck swung the door closed. He hit the horn a couple of times, waved, and pulled the bus back out into the street. He drove on out of town, past the reservoir and up into the cedar-covered hills of central Texas. Austin was about as nice a city as Texas had, but it didn't hold a candle to the country just beyond its limits. Seeing all the people outside the Raw Deal Café had made him miss Viv and Jamie more than he thought possible, and he pressed the accelerator flat against the floor. Then Buck realized that he hadn't brought Viv a present. He jammed on the brakes and pulled over to the shoulder. He had to do something, but he didn't know what.

Buck got his suitcase down, opened it, and began to rifle through all his dirty clothes and belongings. He found what he was looking for—a felt-tip pen given to him by a man who worked at a truck stop. The ink was bright blue. Buck unsnapped his shirt and stood in front of the little mirror that Tex used to comb his hair in a dozen times a day. Carefully he drew big block letters on his chest. The letters said, "Take me, I'm yours." He admired his handiwork when he had finished, then added a couple of hearts and flowers. Then he snapped the shirt closed again.

The words on the mailbox at the end of the one-lane dirt road read Bonham Ranch. Under them was the name, Honeysuckle Rose. It had never been their favorite song. It just represented something precious to them that they couldn't quite explain, a special time, in the beginning, when he and Viv had traveled together. Honeysuckle Rose seemed the best name they could come up with for their own place.

Buck hit the speaker switch above the tape deck, and the music rolled out across his land.

Buck drove around the bend in the road, where it led down to the creek, and saw Jamie standing in the middle of the bridge, his face split by a grin. He turned and ran, and Buck gave chase, leaning on the horn, gunning the engine. He could see the unpainted clapboard house up the creek, a handful of chickens, and a garden so well tended that the beans and the tomato plants stood waist-high. That was Viv for you, he thought. There was no other sign of his wife.

He pulled ahead of Jamie, stopped the bus, and cranked open the door. He jumped down into the weeds, gathered his son up in his arms, and swung him in a wide loop. "Papa, papa," he cried, but for a moment Buck didn't say anything. He held the boy away from him, studying him for any signs of damage that might have occurred while he had been away. Jamie's chestnut-brown hair fell over his eyes, and there was a smudge on his cheek. His clothes were in as poor shape as Buck's, but that was expected of a ten-year-old boy.

"Hey," Buck said, "you weigh a ton. What'ya been eating, cannonballs?" He hugged Jamie again, pressing his face into the boy's hair. "You smell like a cesspool."

"Papa!"

It was true that Jamie had changed subtly in the short time he had been away. Buck felt proud of his son for growing into such a strong, good-looking kid, but he was mystified at the speed of that growth. It seemed no more than a year ago that Jamie couldn't be trusted on the bridge above the creek. Now he was swimming in it.

"Hey," Buck said, "I brought you something for your birthday."

"That was last week."

Buck felt the twinge of guilt again. He had planned to send Jamie a card or telephone him but hadn't gotten around to it. And then the birthday was past.

But Jamie didn't seem to mind. He put his arms around Buck's neck again. "Oh, papa."

Buck carried him onto the bus. He set him down carefully in the aisle, dusted off his hands, and prepared to make magic. Jamie watched him, grinning, expecting him to pull a package out from under the seat, or maybe money out of a shirt pocket, although Buck had only tried that once and had regretted it. The pony stamped a foot behind the blanket, and Jamie jerked his head toward the sound, aware that they weren't alone on the bus. He noticed the mud and manure on the floor. His mouth opened as the possibility began to dawn on him.

Buck swept the blanket aside. "Happy birthday!"

Jamie's eyes widened. He looked from the pony to Buck, unwilling to believe it. Buck nodded, and Jamie ran to the pony, feeling its nose and ears and passing his hands over its withers. Buck felt the guilt and the uncertainty slip away. "Now we've got to get him out of here."

Jamie gave Buck another hug, and for a moment they hung on to one another, happy in their silence. Then Buck handed him the reins and slipped behind the pony. He placed his hands on both flanks, knowing he stood a good chance of getting kicked, and began to push. But the pony was glad to escape. She went down the aisle, took the steps in a bound, and almost landed on Jamie.

Buck climbed onto her back and pulled Jamie up behind him. Buck had once done some rodeoing. He was too skinny to be much good at it, but he knew how to ride a horse. Any horse.

The pony started toward the house at a butt-jarring gait.

"*Yeeeeee-heeeeee!*" shouted Buck.

"*Yaaaaaa-hoooooo!*" shouted Jamie, hugging Buck hard around the middle.

Viv stood on the porch, watching. She wore Levis and a shirt just like Buck's, and she carried a butcher knife carelessly in one hand, brought out from the kitchen. She pushed a pile of strawberry-blond hair out of her eyes, lifting her smiling face to the sun. Buck felt the old tug deep inside of him. He thought his wife was beautiful in the most natural way, lean at forty, and sexier than a woman half her age. She had a wide, friendly mouth, a button nose, and Jamie's deep brown eyes. People sometimes thought of Viv as cute, before they got to know her well.

She called out, "I better get them to deliver some more tequila!"

She dropped the knife and ran down the steps. Buck hooked a boot over the pony's neck and jumped to the ground.

31

"Mama," Jamie said, "look what papa brought me."

Buck caught her up in his arms and held her tightly against him. She smelled of freshly chopped vegetables and a special kind of shampoo she used; she smelled like home. He tried to kiss her, but she was jumping up and down and squealing, and he had to hit a moving target. She tasted even better than she smelled, and he held the kiss until she was breathless.

"I missed you," Viv said, and he knew she meant it. She reared back and looked at his clothes. "What happened to you?"

"That pony was harder to get on the bus than you ever were."

She laughed at the old joke.

"Isn't she pretty, mama?" Jamie ran his hands over the pony, admiring her configuration like an old hand. He patted her haunches. "Look at this rump, mom. Big and wide."

Buck patted Viv's rump approvingly. "Runs in the family, honey."

"I beg your pardon."

She took Buck's hand and brought his arm up to her shoulders. She nuzzled him, encircling his waist with her arm. There was always a touch of shyness in his homecoming, as if they were meeting again for the first time.

Jamie mounted, then rode in a circle around them. Buck noticed that he was good, his back straight and his heels dug into the pony's flanks. "I'm learning to pick, papa. Did mama tell you?"

"Pick what, squirt? Boogers?" Buck couldn't resist teasing him, no matter what the occasion.

"Buck!" Viv scolded.

"The guitar, yo-yo." Teasing Jamie was like spitting into a tin pan—you always got a retort.

"I thought you were going to grow up respectable," Buck said. In fact he was proud that Jamie shared an interest in his instrument.

"Lily's helping me," Jamie said. "She's a great teacher."

"Lily?"

"Garland's girl," Viv said.

"Oh, yeah." She was one of the reasons Garland was quitting the band.

"She's a good musician."

"Garland's daughter," Buck said. "She ought'a be."

"Well, she is."

Jamie was still riding circles around them. "I bet she can flat out shit-an'-git, all right."

Buck didn't know if he was talking about the pony or Garland's daughter. "What kind'a talk is that?"

"That's hired hand talk," Viv said. "He's been hanging around the men cutting our hay."

"I'm gonna stretch her out," Jamie said. "See you later, papa."

He spun the pony and galloped through the gate, his dark hair flying. He went straight across the bridge, the pony's hoofs pounding the old boards. That bridge needed propping up, and from where he stood Buck could see half a dozen pieces of fence that needed mending. He should be cutting his own hay himself. There were a hundred things to do that required a man's talents and a man's strength and time, and all Buck could think about was Garland retiring.

"Well," Viv said, sensing that something was wrong, "welcome home, lover."

Buck nodded approvingly and kissed her flat on the forehead. "Yeah," he said, feeling a sudden weariness and the weight of all his traveling.

"Seems like these wars are getting longer every time."

Viv tightened her grip around his waist and turned him toward the house.

"Let's go have a look at those wounds."

They went up the steps together and through the door. The familiarity of the house was so complete that he felt he had never left, or had been gone a day or two at most. The long road and all the engagements Buck had played on the tour faded into the past. The sensation wasn't totally agreeable. If he could forget so quickly, then how real would his singing and picking seem to him a year after he retired? Or after five years? Garland was crazy to give it up if he didn't have to.

But there was no getting around it, home was nice. Buck stopped in the middle of the floor and took in the stone fireplace with the rack of antlers above it—what cowboy's sitting room could do without them?—and the Apache saddle blanket hanging on the wall, the lamp he had made out of an old wagon hub, and Jamie's bronzed baby shoes. The framed photographs on the wall showed Buck playing with Viv, with Garland and some of the band members who were no longer part of the group. Looking at them now made Buck feel old.

They went on into the bedroom, as they had done on a hundred previous homecomings. Buck sat down on the edge of the brass bed, on the brightly colored quilt that Viv had found time to stitch together since she had stopped traveling with the band. He ran his hand affectionately over the material, while Viv stepped to the window to make sure Jamie hadn't been thrown. They could hear him laughing and calling out from the road.

Buck began to struggle with a boot. He liked wearing boots except right before he made love.

Then it seemed they were particularly hard to get off.

"Let me do that," Viv said.

"It's okay."

He didn't want her to get her hands dirty, but she placed a finger on his forehead and gently pushed him back on the mattress. Buck let her worry with the boot. As she did she looked down at him in loving appraisal, and he knew she was glad to have her old man home. The truth was, he was glad to be home, too.

"Sometimes I wonder why me and everyone else makes such a fuss over you," she said. "You're just a scraggly, redneck, lippy cowboy singer that needs a haircut and a shave and has to drink a beer to keep his pants up."

Buck glanced over his shoulder, as if a bartender stood there ready to serve him. "Hold that beer," he said. "These things are coming off, anyway."

Viv pulled the boot off. She held it up, sniffed, and wrinkled her nose. But Buck didn't laugh.

"Something wrong?" she asked.

"Garland's quittin' on me. Rosella tell you about that?"

Rosella was Garland's wife, the only one he had ever had. Buck knew that she and Viv were closer than two cows in the same chute, and it was hard to believe that Viv hadn't heard something.

"Point your toes," was all she said. Buck did as he was told, but he suspected that his wife was avoiding the question. She jerked off the second boot, after expertly working it back and forth to free the high arch. She set the pair out in the hall, then went to wash her hands in the bathroom. Buck figured she was trying to think of something encouraging to say.

"Leaves a pretty big hole in the band," he called to her.

Viv came back drying her hands in a towel, avoiding his eyes. "That's too bad. What are you gonna do about it?"

"Gonna buy you a new guitar, I guess."

She still wouldn't look at him, but he knew she had gotten the hint. Buck would have loved to get her back out on the road, although his past attempts had all failed. Maybe she would have to come now.

"It ain't so much his pickin' I'll miss," he said, "as the companionship."

She knelt on the bed and leaned over him. "I just happen to have a bunch of that"—she paused to kiss him softly, moistly on the lips—"companionship"—she kissed him again, lingering—"right here."

Buck forgot all about Garland. He reached up and took hold of the top of her cowboy shirt. "Where?" he asked. "Lemme see."

He opened the top snap. Both their breaths quickened. Buck could feel her bosom swell against his hand. Viv didn't wear see-through blouses, but she had as fine a chest as those groupies who hung around the stage during concerts or filled up the motel corridors. More important, she didn't share it with every harmonica player, guitar picker and drummer who came along. Viv was his woman, not just his wife.

He reached for the second snap, but she took his hand in hers, slowing down the process. Viv had a great sense of timing.

"You're a little shaky there, cowboy. You been drinking?"

"No. Thinkin' about you." He hadn't made love to her in almost a month. That was a long time between drinks—enough to make any man's hands shake.

"Yeah," she whispered. "I know how that goes."

She took the top of his shirt in both hands and pulled. The snaps came loose in rapid succession. She stared down at the message inked on her husband's chest, and Buck watched the delight come into her eyes. Then she put her head back and howled with laughter.

"Now it's my turn," he said.

He touched the bottom snap on her shirt. "Hmmm, I think I'll try this one." He popped it open and slipped his hand inside, touching her belly. The skin was smooth and warm. Buck rose up on one elbow, feeling the blood rush to his throat and ears. Viv moaned and stretched, like a cat under his touch, her eyes closed. He could see her navel, and the downy hair that ringed it, and he leaned forward and kissed her there.

Viv took hold of the bottom of her shirt, to finish what Buck had started. The snaps gave way, and her breasts swung free. He buried his face in them, kissing one taut nipple and then the other. Viv continued to moan. She ran her hands over his shoulders and chest and down over the flat of his stomach, to the hardness of his crotch.

His Levis had grown very uncomfortable. He pulled her down onto the bed and rose above her, tugging at his belt.

"Papa!"

It was Jamie. He knocked on the door and called again, impatient as only a kid could be. Buck looked down at his wife, remembering for an instant what it had once been like to make love all afternoon, without interruption. She smiled in sympathy, and he knew she remembered, too.

"Excuse me a second," he said.

Buck went to the door. Before opening it, he reached in his pocket and took out a plastic card that he had saved just for the occasion. He had picked it up at a Holiday Inn where the band had spent a night, and he held it up for Viv's inspection. The card said DO NOT DISTURB.

"See?" he said playfully. "I ain't as dumb as I look."

He opened the door just wide enough to get his arm through. Jamie stood in the hall, watching, his hands deep in the pockets of his jeans.

"Sorry, papa. But I—"

"What's wrong with you?" Buck asked, pretending to be angry. He showed Jamie the sign and then hung it on the doorknob. "Can't you read the sign? Go feed your pony."

Jamie started to protest, but Buck held up his hand and raised his nose, like a rich guest in a fancy hotel. "I'll be out in a couple of minutes."

Jamie watched the door close. The emotions he felt were strong and confusing. He thought the sign was funny. He was glad to have his father home, and he was more grateful for the pony than for any gift he had ever received. But he was also disappointed that his father didn't want to spend the first few hours with him, and jealous of both his parents. Of his mother for giving the attention he was accustomed to receiving to Buck, of his father for shutting him out in favor of Viv, although he knew the relationship between a man and a woman was different. No boy his age who had grown up on a ranch didn't know the difference. It went with the territory, as Buck would say.

"Couple of minutes, my ass," Jamie whispered.

He took the sign off the doorknob, turned it

around, and replaced it. Now it read: MAID SER-VICE, Pl ase Clean This Room Immediately.

Jamie had an idea. "Wish we had a maid!" he shouted. Laughing, he ran down the hall and out into the sunlight.

5

Like most country people, they ate supper
long before dark. After the meal was done and the
dishes washed, Buck stepped out onto the porch
and took up his usual stance, one shoulder propped
against a post, his boots crossed. The evening air
smelled clean and moist. The sun was gone, but
light lingered about the crests of the hills in the
distance, pink in the bare spots, and gray where the
cedar grew. Some of those hills were owned by
Buck's relatives. There were Bonhams all over the
county, and beyond, and he liked the feeling of
living close to his own folks, on land that had been
theirs for generations.

The lower meadow filled up with shadow. He
could see the hay bales scattered over the pasture
like geometrical children's blocks. The hired men
hadn't bothered to pick them up, knowing it
wouldn't rain and spoil the hay before they returned in the morning to finish the job. The bales
would be stacked in the barn, and Buck wouldn't
have to buy feed for the two milk cows—and the
pony—until the following spring.

As he watched, the bales began to disappear,
one by one, consumed by the darkness. A lopsided
moon hung way out over Austin, gaining in brilliance. He heard the tree frogs first—a high shrill-
ing so constant that it took him a while to realize

he was listening to it. The crickets were next. The sing-song chirruping seemed to come from the grass at the foot of the steps, but when Buck shifted his boots, the sound jumped over to the corner of the house. Pretty soon he couldn't tell where it was coming from. The bullfrogs started their ponderous croaking, secure on the mud bank above the creek, irregular but louder than all the others combined.

Buck saw a light blink on at the far end of the road, weaving like a lantern carried by a drunk. It went out, then came on again halfway across the pasture. Suddenly there were a dozen lanterns, all blinking and weaving. Fireflies, he thought. The best part of summer.

Viv joined Buck on the porch. She shut the screen door softly behind her, and the hinges squeaked.

"Don't do that," Buck said.

"What?"

"Open it up and let go of it."

She looked at him warily, trying to understand him. She opened the screen door as far as it would go and let it clap shut.

Buck grinned at her. She said, "You feeling all right?"

"I haven't heard a screen door slam or smelled fresh-cut hay all summer."

He took another deep breath. Then he pulled Viv to him and pushed his face into her hair. "Or you," he added.

The screen door clapped again. Carrying a big Mason jar, Jamie crossed the porch and started down the steps. He pretended that his parents weren't there.

"Where are you going, mister?" Viv asked. "It's past your bedtime."

"I'm gonna catch fireflies." He raced off, not

41

waiting for permission. "Just gimme a couple of minutes."

They watched him gambol on the lawn. Jamie reminded Buck of the colt—all legs and enthusiasm. He would rush up to a firefly, make a scooping motion toward it with the jar, and slap his hand over the mouth. The quarry eluded him as often as not. When the jar was full to his satisfaction, he would take it into Buck's room and release the fireflies. That was Jamie's favorite prank.

"Want to help him catch some?" Buck asked.

"No," Viv said, "I got to finish making that potato salad for tomorrow."

That was a big job, all right, making potato salad for all the Bonhams. The family reunion to be held at the county hall the next day was the event of the summer. The party wouldn't be limited to Bonhams, but would include all the friends and relatives and would develop into a real foot-stomping, beer-drinking good time, with music, food, and plenty of romancing. What Garland called a shit-kicker. Buck was looking forward to it.

But Viv seemed reluctant to go back inside the house. She said, "Do you sleep with many other women when you're out on the road, Buck?"

He wasn't prepared for that. Viv had never asked such a thing before, and the question hung in front of them like a thundercloud. Their lovemaking that afternoon had been good, and prolonged, and he wondered why she doubted him now.

Buck decided to tell the truth. "No, I don't."

"Not many," she said, "or none at all?"

He looked down at his wife, searching for an indication of her mood. But Viv's features were hidden in the darkness. He felt anger stirring inside of him and the beginnings of apprehension. He didn't like to have his life questioned, but he knew that Viv had her reasons, that she was not a careless person. He also knew that there was fire in her, smoldering at times and difficult to detect if you didn't know her, but a real force in her personality. She could be as fierce and as unpredictable as Buck himself. And once she made up her mind, there was no changing it.

Before he could answer, she said, "I was feeling blue the other night, and I had a glass of wine. Three, actually. And"—she paused while Jamie ran past the steps—"you had left a joint laying on your desk. So I smoked it."

"You?" Buck was surprised. Viv never smoked pot, and she rarely drank.

"Yeah. Little ol' me."

Now Buck wanted to ask the questions. Had Viv gone honky-tonking in Austin? Had she slept with one of the hired men? He knew she hadn't, but he felt uncomfortable with the possibility.

"I don't see how you could possibly smoke that stuff very often," she said, "and not want to go to bed with somebody . . . when you're all alone."

He didn't know what to say. Viv was right, of course; she usually was. It occurred to him that loneliness—and adultery—was a two-way street.

"I gotta go slice up potatoes."

She went inside and let the screen door slam behind her.

"Look!" Jamie called to him. "I got a mess of 'em." He held up the Mason jar, which glowed with a pale, greenish light.

"Hey, papa, I want to show you something."

He bounded up the steps and took Buck's hand. Jamie led him through the door, across the living room, and down the hall to his room. He set the Mason jar on the floor. A toy airplane hung from a wire attached to the ceiling, and Jamie switched on the battery-run device with barely a glance at it. Viv had given it to him for his birthday, and he turned it on automatically, as if it were a radio, every time he walked into his room. Buck was amused by the authority with which Jamie operated on his own turf. He pointed to the bed, and Buck obediently sat. The airplane flew in a tight circle around the room, just above Jamie's head, but he paid it no attention. He was more interested in the guitar standing in the corner.

The walls were covered with posters of horses, World War II airplanes, and Buck Bonham's Band. Buck's face peered out of half a dozen different photographs taken during concerts. Buck was flattered by his son's approval but uncertain of his own response. Buck wasn't sure that he wanted Jamie to grow up being a musician.

Jamie brought the guitar over and sat down next to him. The instrument was old and the frets worn, but it had a good sound. Buck had bought it the year before because it was small enough for Jamie to handle. Buck had not expected him to learn to tune and play it so quickly. Jamie made a lot of mistakes, but he was a dedicated picker.

He set his fingers on the strings and began to play "Blue Moon of Kentucky." He tried to play it, anyway, but only Buck would have recognized the tune. Jamie got wilder and wilder, until he missed a chord.

"Oooops," he said, glancing at Buck.

"Here, you missed this one."

Buck rearranged his fingers on the frets. Jamie played it again. "Oh, yeah, there it is," he said, when he came to the crucial chord. But then he missed another.

"Aw, shoot."

"That's all right, you're gettin' it." Buck knew how easy it was to get discouraged learning the guitar. Playing came so naturally to him that he

44

had never given it a thought, but he had seen other people struggle over the strings for years.

Jamie began the song again, his tongue between his teeth, playing with more care. He had been close to tears, but now he was smiling, the music filling his small room.

"Don't stop," Buck said. "You got it now. Yessir!"

He looked up and saw Viv standing in the doorway, watching them both with obvious satisfaction.

6

The county hall stood at the end of the packed dirt road, an elemental structure painted white years before. Mesquite trees nestled around it, offering some relief from the sun, and the windows were open, in anticipation of a breeze. Most days the hall looked isolated and a little forlorn, lost in the middle of the landscape, and without any real purpose. But not that day. Dozens of pickups and old battered sedans were parked haphazardly in the yard, and a banner stretched above the door read, in bold red and blue letters, 52ND ANNUAL BONHAM FAMILY REUNION. Tables made of plywood sheets set on sawhorses were covered with red-and-white checkered cloths, and women in clean aprons moved among them, setting out tubs of three-bean salad and cole slaw, stacks of silverware rolled in white paper napkins, jars of chili peppers and steaksauce. Brisquets of beef and fresh pork sausage sizzled on grills over the charcoal fires.

Buck smelled the cooking meat from half a mile away. He drove his pickup slowly, Viv snuggled against him. Her sister Jessie, a plainer version of Viv who had begun to get thick around the middle, rode shotgun. All three of them were eager to get to the party, but Jamie had followed them on the pony, and Buck wouldn't rush it. He could see the domino boards set out under the live oak trees; several games were already in progress. A crowd of men stood around the beer stand, grabbing for cans of Pearl and Lone Star, and several of them shouted as Buck drove up.

He parked close to the hall so Viv and Jessie wouldn't have far to carry the potato salad riding in the truck bed in big covered dishes. Jamie went galloping off, chased by a dozen kids who wanted a look at the pony. The sounds of a Texas swing band and the scraping of feet against the bare floorboards poured out the open windows. The dancing had already started.

Garland and Rosella came to meet them. Garland had shined up his inlaid belt buckle for the occasion, and his stomach lapped over the top of it. Rosella wore a calico party dress, her hair tied up in a bright green ribbon, and she looked happier than Buck could ever remember.

She put her arms around him and squeezed. "I didn't figure you'd let him quit, Buck."

"Hell," he said playfully, squeezing her back, "I was about to fire him, anyway. His bones got to creaking so loud it was interrupting the music."

Rosella went to Viv and hugged her. "Jamie sure looks cute on that pony."

"Don't he?" Viv held the older woman at arm's length, inspecting her. "You look like a mighty happy woman, Rosella."

"Oh, I am."

Buck felt uncomfortable with all the rejoicing. Avoiding Garland's eyes, he watched Jessie carry a covered dish toward the picnic tables.

"Ya'll come on," he said finally, taking his wife and Rosella by the arms. "Let's go drink to the good times."

As soon as they entered the hall, they were besieged by friends and relatives. Buck shook hands with and hugged people he hadn't seen for a year, or longer, and he was able to put Garland's quitting out of his mind. Men he had grown up with joshed Buck, laughing and tugging at his pigtails. Buck was a star—an outlandish and successful country musician—but he was also part of the home folks. Some of his relatives didn't approve of the way he looked and behaved, but they all seemed to like him well enough.

Viv pulled him out onto the dance floor and held him in the classical pose. They swept around the room. Buck saw Bo and Bliss standing in a corner, tipping up their beers, and laughing. He had invited the entire band to the reunion, as he did every year, but he wasn't sure he liked to have his bass players commenting on his dancing. Buck almost collided with an old woman who was shaking cornmeal from a bag onto the floor, to keep it slick. Two boys streaked past, one of them pulling the other on a burlap sack. The musicians on the stage had seen Buck. They called out to him and raised their beers, and Buck waved back.

It was too hot in the hall, and the four of them went back out into the shade of the oaks. Buck and Garland worked their way up to the bar, pulling the women behind them. The bartender's name was Owen, a good-natured farmer wearing a Cat driver's hat, already full of beer himself. He offered his hand and Buck shook it.

"How you doin', Buck?"

"Ain't nobody throwin' rocks at me, Owen."

"That's a change, ain't it?"

Owen howled with laughter. He set several beers on the bar and took one for himself. After paying for them, Buck passed the beers around, then tipped his back. The cold beer whetted his appetite. He was already sweating, happy in the good dry heat of July in the hill country. He could see Jamie and three other boys sneaking up on the outdoor privy behind the hall. One of the boys lit a firecracker and dropped it through the half-moon cutout in the door. Buck heard a muffled explosion. The boys ran off, Jamie giggling so hard that Buck thought he would stumble, but he didn't.

The door flapped open, and a man stepped out, holding up his trousers and cursing. The domino players all laughed at him.

Viv led Buck deeper into the shade, to the spot where Grandpa Bonham was holding court. He sat in a rocker, wearing a hearing aid and a string tie with a polished agate clasp, receiving all the relatives. For years that had been his place on reunion day, beneath the big oak, a chew of Bull Durham in one cheek, his wife at his side to do the mediating. Grandpa Bonham had cataracts and didn't see too well; he remembered less.

Buck went through the same ritual every summer. He bent close to the old man and shouted, "Hello, grandpa!"

"Who're you?"

His wife said, "That's Buck, grandpa." She smiled understandingly at Buck. "You know, Olean's boy."

Grandpa Bonham scrutinized Buck's hair and beard. "What do you do for a living, Buck?"

"I play guitar, grandpa."

"Yeah." The old man nodded, as if music making was all Buck was good for. His pale blue eyes blinked as he tried to place his grandson. His wife patted his hand. She was not Buck's real grandmother, since Grandpa Bonham had remarried years before. Buck's own mother and father were both dead, and grandpa was the only direct link between Buck and the memory of his father.

"I don't think the sawmill'd have you," grandpa said, "looking like that."

49

Buck laughed and squeezed his knee. He stepped back, to let the woman who had gathered around take the old man's picture with their Polaroids. Grandpa was almost one hundred years old, and every reunion was expected to be his last.

As Buck followed Viv toward the serving tables, he heard grandpa say, "So that's Olean's boy."

"Yep," said his wife.

"Who's Olean?"

They had to wait in line for the food. Buck hailed Sid, who stood watching the domino games. He came over, trailed by a man named Eubanks, one of the best domino players in the county.

"There's an empty table over yonder," Eubanks said, grabbing Sid's arm.

"All right." Sid glanced at Buck and shrugged. It wasn't poker, but it was better than nothing.

"I generally play two dollars a game," Eubanks said. "Don't hurt nobody much that way."

It sounded like Sid was being suckered. But then Eubanks didn't know about Sid's way with numbers.

Buck picked up a plate. The serving tables had been loaded with trays of barbequed beef and pork, braised ribs and sausage, calf brains spooned up out of an actual calf's skull with the top sawed off, and tamales wrapped in corn husks. There were tubs of steaming sauerkraut, roasted corn, and whole potatoes. Real Texas chili bubbled in a caldron set over a Sterno flame, the smell of red peppers so strong that Buck could taste them. Platters of fried chicken, steaks, pork chops, and french fries covered one whole table. There were freshly sliced tomatoes sprinkled with tarragon, cold string beans in vinegar, lady peas cooked with fatback, and stewed onions. The dessert table was crowded with cakes with chocolate or coconut frosting, thick, rich brownies, apple and custard pies, rice pudding, and ginger snaps. Buck didn't know where to begin.

"Gimme that plate, you skinny thing." His sister-in-law jerked it out of his hand. "Man, you're looking like a peeled twig."

Jessie marched down the tables, loading Buck's plate with meat and vegetables of every variety. Pretty soon she had the food piled so high that Buck thought it would start an avalanche. People were always telling him to eat, to take care of himself. He did take care of himself when he was home with Viv and Jamie, but when he was on the road, it was hard to eat and sleep regularly. Much of the time it was impossible.

He saw Jamie walking between the picnic tables. He started to wave him over, but then Jamie went up to a young woman and put his arms around her neck. That surprised Buck. Jamie wasn't fond of hugging women, even pretty ones. She was in her early twenties, he guessed, with long dark hair, and soft—almost childish—features. She wore Levis, boots, and a cowboy shirt, but there was a gentleness in her manner often missing from the girls who attended the Bonham reunions. This girl had a way of her own. Buck tried to place her, but he couldn't.

He walked over to them and put out his hand. "I'm Jamie's daddy."

The girl laughed at his formality.

"I'm Lily," she said.

"Lily?" He didn't know a Lily.

"Papa, I told you about Lily last night. She's my guitar teacher."

"I'm Garland's daughter," she said.

Buck's surprise wasn't totally agreeable. Everything seemed to lead back to Garland, reminding Buck that he was quitting. Lily was too old and too good-looking to be the daughter of a close friend of his. The last time he had seen her, she was a child.

"Well, I'll be damned," he said, feeling foolish. "You've done a lot of growin'."

"Well, you haven't seen me in three years."

Ten years seemed more likely. She just smiled, showing him perfectly white, perfectly straight teeth. Buck just couldn't believe it.

"I've been away at school," she added.

"Three years? Nah." Buck looked her over again. Garland and Rosella had taken good care of her, that was for sure.

Jamie took Lily's hand and led her off toward the chow line. She seemed reluctant to take her eyes off Buck's.

Garland, Rosella, and Viv were calling him. He went over and took a seat in front of the mountain of food that Jessie had collected for him. They ate quickly, listening to the music coming from inside the hall and waving to friends. Buck commented on Viv's potato salad, and Garland commented on Rosella's peach pie. Otherwise, they didn't talk much.

Buck worked on his portion until he had made a sizable dent in the food and then pushed the plate away. He bought beers for himself and Garland, but the women refused. Then they went back into the hall and danced to the swing music. It was the only alternative to falling asleep under the live oaks. People constantly circulated between the hall and the food tables, the bar, the domino games, and the patches of soft grass beyond the trees, where the younger children romped. Jamie wasn't with them now. Jessie had collared him and dragged him onto the dance floor, and Jamie, his arm around his aunt's ample waist, waltzed back and forth looking unhappy. Buck tried not to laugh when Jamie scowled at him.

The music trailed off, and everybody applauded. Buck had left his beer in the open window, and he was on his way to get it when he heard the band leader say, into the microphone, "Hey, Buck, come sing us a song."

Buck had expected the request. The band didn't play Buck's kind of music, and the band leader wasn't Buck's type, but they were kin. The band leader wore his hair oiled and combed back. His ranch suit was black with white stitching, his lacquered white boots too shiny to look at. He wore a little red scarf around his neck fastened with a gold ring set with a big turquoise.

Buck climbed up onto the stage and shook his hand. All the faces were turned toward him, and more people were crowding in from outside, carrying beer cans and chunks of cake, anxious to hear some real picking and singing. Buck felt the old excitement of performing, even there at the Bonham family reunion. There were no two ways about it—he just loved to play to a crowd, to show them what he could do and feel them respond.

Then he saw Jamie standing in front of his mother, grinning up at Buck, and he had an idea.

"All right, ya'll," Buck announced. "Today's a special day. It's the first time Jamie Bonham's gonna play guitar in front of an audience."

Everyone applauded. Jamie's mouth fell open; he looked like he wanted to slip through a crack in the floor. Buck jumped down from the stage and took his hand. "What do you say, son?"

Jamie tried to pull away, but Buck wouldn't release him. He knew Jamie would like to play, once he got started. Buck coaxed him toward the stage. They climbed up together, and Buck set him on the stool, in front of the mike. He took a guitar from one of the musicians and handed it to Jamie, then felt his heart sink. The guitar was much too big.

Everyone was waiting. Buck took the band leader's guitar for himself and struck a chord. He winked at Jamie, but his son still looked panicked. He was searching the audience for someone, and Buck realized it was Lily, his teacher. She stood between Garland and Rosella, smiling encouragingly at Jamie, nodding and motioning for him to play. Jamie waved her toward the stage. Buck was surprised to see Lily take her own guitar from a case in the corner and with graceful ease climb onto the stage.

Buck began to play the introduction to one of his favorite songs, "Crazy." Lily and Jamie came in with him. For a while they were in perfect harmony, and Buck looked down to see Viv watching them, pure satisfaction on her face. He was glad she could see how much he loved and enjoyed being with Jamie, who was picking for all he was worth. But the neck of the guitar was too thick, and eventually he missed a chord. Lily quickly reached down and set his fingers right; Buck didn't even have to stop playing.

He stepped forward, bent to the mike, and began to sing.

> Crazy, crazy for feeling so lonely,
> I'm crazy, crazy for feeling so blue.

Jamie missed another chord. This time he stopped playing.

"You're all right," Buck whispered. "Keep going."

Jamie's eyes filled with tears, but he kept right

on playing. Buck knew he was going to be all right, and he turned his full attention to the song.

> I know you'd love me
> As long as you wanted . . .

This time Buck didn't turn around when Jamie missed a chord; he didn't want to embarrass him. He sang on, waiting for the accompaniment to start up again.

When it did, Buck wasn't prepared for the strength and clarity of Jamie's playing. Surprised, he turned around and saw that it wasn't Jamie with the borrowed guitar, but Lily. The stool where Jamie had sat was empty.

Buck saw him race across the floor and out the front door. Confused, he looked down at Viv, who jerked her head in his direction. Buck would have to go after him. He set the guitar against a chair and jumped off the stage. People made way for him. Buck paused before going outside and looked back. Lily continued to play his song and to sing it; Buck hadn't heard that kind of talent in a long time. She sounded just like Garland might, if he had been a girl.

Buck walked among the oaks. He saw Jamie far ahead of him, running down toward the river, the sunlight bright on his hair. By the time Buck reached him, he was sitting on a rock that extended out into the water, his knees drawn up under his chin. He didn't acknowledge Buck's arrival but stared off across the river, toward home. Here the sound of the music barely reached them. A group of boys in their undershorts were swimming in the tea-colored water further upstream, but Buck and Jamie were alone. Buck was glad for that.

He sat down next to Jamie but said nothing. He was sorry he had pushed the boy into a performance before he was ready, and he didn't know how to make amends.

"I messed up your song," Jamie said, and he began to cry again.

"Naw, shoot, you were blending right in."

Jamie looked up shyly, and they both smiled. The boy had a wonderful way of bouncing back.

"Listen," Buck said, "everybody makes mistakes. I make 'em all the time." That was true enough. "You were up there trying—that's what counts."

"I don't have any music in me, papa."

It was a sad admission, and one Buck couldn't accept—not from his own son.

"Everybody's got music in 'em."

"Not me," Jamie insisted.

"'Course you do. You're my son, ain't ya? Everything you ever heard, everything you ever saw, or touched"—Buck poked him gently in the stomach, and Jamie giggled—"it's all in there bubbling and churning around. After a while it'll make some music if you'll give it a chance. You'll see."

Jamie dried his eyes. "How do you get it to come out, papa?"

"I don't. I just let it happen. The music just stumbles and falls out on its own. Sometimes, anyway." He paused, trying to be honest about a process he really didn't understand. Sometimes the music came in on wings, when he was traveling. Sometimes Buck had to sweat it out.

"Sometimes you have to work real hard to get it out," he said.

He put his arm around Jamie's frail shoulders. The two of them sat there in silence, looking out over the water. The sound of the boys swimming reached them; suddenly Buck had an inspiration.

"Hey," he said, "last one in's a rotten egg."

Buck jumped up and started to unsnap his shirt. Jamie, grinning, did the same, the performance forgotten. He loved a race, and he loved to swim. Most of all, he loved being with his dad.

Buck waited until Jamie was halfway out of his shirt, then turned and jumped into the river. The last thing he saw, before he went under the cool water, was Jamie's astonished expression. Buck came up spitting and coughing. It wasn't easy, swimming with all his clothes on and his boots. Jamie squealed and jumped in after him. The two of them splashed around together, Buck supporting him, until they were gasping for breath.

They pulled themselves up on the rock and lay drying in the sun. The boys who had been swimming upstream came down to look at them, unable to believe Buck and Jamie had done it on purpose. The boys would have been whipped if they had gotten their best clothes soaked. Buck knew that Viv wouldn't be too happy about it, either. He turned and squinted toward the hall and saw that people were watching for more antics.

They headed up the hill, Buck with his hand on Jamie's shoulder. They passed Sid and Eubanks playing dominoes in the shade. A stack of one-dollar bills stood in front of Sid; old man Eubanks didn't look too happy.

Viv stood outside the hall, her arms crossed, trying to look angry. Garland was talking to her from inside the hall, leaning out the open window.

"Don't do no good to get yourself worked up," he told Viv.

"I know." She looked at Buck and Jamie and shook her head.

"That's the way he is," Garland said. "Ain't nothing gonna change him."

57

To prove Garland's words, Buck took off a boot and poured water into the dust. Jamie did the same thing.

"Will you look at that." Garland put his head back and laughed. "What was I tellin' ya?"

"And I keep waiting for him to grow up," Viv said.

"He was silly when you married him, and he's gonna die silly."

A group of boys had gathered round. "Hey, Jamie, come on."

Jamie looked up at Buck for permission, and he nodded. Jamie took off.

"Jamie!" Viv called. "You stop! You're soaking wet!"

She ran after him and grabbed him by a leg. Jamie tried to get free, playfully, knowing that he was really caught. Buck would let him do what he wanted, but Viv would never let him run around in that condition. "You need some dry clothes," she said.

Buck decided that it was time for another beer. He went over to the bar, where Owen was trading the icy cans for money, and not bothering to count it. He seemed pretty far gone to Buck for so early in the day, but that was the way Owen operated. He handed Buck a fresh Pearl without having to be asked, then pushed his money back across the frothy surface of the bar.

Buck was about to take a swallow when he felt someone tugging at his pants leg. He looked down and saw three boys hidden beneath the bar, watching the men drink. They were older than Jamie, but not much older. They grinned, showing crooked teeth, gesturing toward Buck's beer. He wondered why people, and dogs and kids, always figured him to be the outlaw. He looked around to make sure no responsible adults were watching and then stooped down and handed his can to one of the boys. They disappeared under the bar, and a second later he saw them running off among the tables, tussling with his Pearl.

Buck held up empty hands for Owen to see. Owen stared, belched with great satisfaction, and handed Buck another beer. He still wouldn't take his money.

Lily sat off by herself at one of the tables, watching Buck and nursing her own beer. That was another thing he couldn't get used to—Garland's daughter drinking right out there in front of everybody.

He walked up to her and said, "Mind if I join you?"

"Not at all." She smiled at the sight of his clothes; it seemed like he was always amusing this young woman. "What happened to you?"

"Been swimming." Buck sat down and took a long pull on the can. There was nothing like drinking beer in the hot Texas sun. Buck knew men who did nothing else. "Where'd you learn to play like that, Lily?"

"Listening to your records."

"You must have pretty good ears," Buck said, though he was flattered. "It never sounded that good to me."

"Bullshit."

Again she had surprised him, this time by cursing and making it sound so sweet and natural. "What d'ya mean?" He really wanted to know.

"I know *I'm* pretty good," Lily told him. "*You* must know you're great."

Buck took another swallow to cover his embarrassment. "Your daddy's great. He's gonna be hard to replace."

Lily seemed to know all about Garland's quitting. "Well," she said, "when are you goin' out again?"

"In a few days. I have to finish this summer tour."

They sat listening to the music coming from the hall. People had begun to dance again, and the domino games had become serious. The party would go on all night, if the food and the beer lasted. Buck wondered vaguely if Lily had a boyfriend. A girl that pretty, and that good on the guitar, probably had a dozen.

"Why don't you take me, Buck? I'm not doing anything this summer."

"On the road?" The thought would never have occurred to him. But he thought of the way Lily had looked standing on that stage—and the way she had sounded. "Nah, you don't want a career in music." He felt he ought to discourage her.

"Yes, I do," she said. "And besides, it's just finishing the summer tour." She set her beer down and leaned toward him across the table. She wasn't laughing now, her dark eyes narrowed, intent. "I could learn a lot, Buck."

He sighed and looked away. Lily was a natural player, as Buck was, but she was also Garland's daughter. "No, it'd break your daddy's heart. He's stayin' home for you—"

Buck knew he shouldn't have said that. But this girl got him flustered. The truth was, she had a good idea. "Partly, anyway," he added. "And you got more school—"

"I'd give that up to play with you."

"No." Buck had a lot of people wanting to join his band. He knew how to sound final, even when he didn't want to. "I can't do that to Garland."

Lily stood up. "You hypocrite."

60

Buck looked up at her with real surprise. That was one thing that he had never been called.

"You don't even listen to your own songs," Lily said, and she walked away, toward the dance hall.

Buck watched her go, unsure of his emotions.

7

The daylight seeped away. Tex looked out the window of the dance hall and saw a bunch of boys, Jamie Bonham among them, chasing an armadillo down the hill, into the setting sun. By the time they came up again, it was dark outside, the lights in the hall casting long shadows on the ground. Some of the men had built a fire there and suspended a huge cast-iron coffee pot from a tripod. People stood around the fire, joking, swapping stories, and drinking the thick black camp coffee to keep awake for the long night ahead, or to sober up a bit. A steady stream of men and women, girls and boys flowed between the dance hall and the outside tables, where bare electric bulbs dangled from wires strung among the branches of the oaks.

Buck had taken over the stage, replacing the swing band, and his familiar, ringing voice had packed the dance floor.

The song, "Funny How Time Slips Away," was one of Tex's favorites. He couldn't hear it without wanting to play the drums, or at least move to the rhythm. It also made him feel amorous, but then most songs did. Jeannie had gone off to the powder room, and he took advantage of her absence to ask a big-breasted country girl to dance. She had been giving him the eye, and when he walked over to her, she just turned and put an arm around his neck, as if they were old friends. That was one good thing about playing in Buck's band—people just naturally felt they knew you.

Tex moved the girl around the floor, pressing her breasts against his chest.

Kelly brushed against them, in the arms of a young girl. While Tex watched, another girl came up and broke in. Kelly had his pick of the babies, Tex thought; he was a cradle robber. Kelly couldn't handle a real woman, not like Tex could.

How's your new love?
I hope that he's doin' fine.
Heard that you told him you'd love him
'Til the end of time.

Buck might have been singing just to Tex and the girl in his arms. He leaned down and told her, in a whisper, that he would like to take a stroll with her behind the hall. He said it in a joshing way, but they both knew he was serious. Unfortunately, before she could answer, Tex noticed Jeannie standing at the edge of the crowd, frowning and watching him like a hawk.

The song ended. Tex gave his partner an extra squeeze, reinforcing the proposition he had made, and drifted back toward his date.

"Don't dance with her no more," Jeannie said, pouting.

"Aw, Jeannie." He played innocent, but she wasn't buying that act.

"Just don't, you hear!"

Viv had joined Buck on the stage, and the two of them began to sing their favorite song, "Loving Her Was Easier Than Anything I'll Ever Do Again", face-to-face in front of the mike, their lips inches apart. Everyone knew it was the song they had sung when they had traveled on the road together. Hearing it was just like old times. When their voices came together, it was like the strains of one instrument.

Tex stole a glance back at the big-breasted girl. She winked at him and headed for the door.

"Oh, damn," Tex said, as sorrowfully as he could. "I made you feel bad. Lemme go get you a beer, honey."

Jeannie thought about the offer and then nodded. There wasn't too much trouble Tex could get into between her and the bar.

Tex knew differently, of course. He hurried out into the night, but there was no sign of the girl with the big breasts. Maybe she had misunderstood his directions. He stepped up to the bar and ordered two beers. Owen was having trouble getting the beers open. His eyes wouldn't focus. Tex had to help him make change, he was so drunk. A cup of coffee stood steaming on the bar, set there by Owen's wife in an attempt to straighten him out, but Owen spiked it with some bourbon from a bottle in his back pocket.

Tex saw the girl he'd danced with standing beyond the tables, at the edge of the light, her arms crossed, cradling her breasts. She smiled at him and then disappeared into the darkness.

He picked up the beers and went after her. Tex had a weakness for girls built like that; he couldn't help himself. Jeannie was well endowed, but Tex couldn't resist the promise of some strange stuff, as he and the boys in the band called it.

It was pitch black now beyond the ring of tables. Tex stumbled, dropping one of the beers. He walked straight into a leafy branch. There was no sign of the girl in the white party dress.

"Psst!" he called. "Pssssssst!"

She answered from further down the hill. He

took another swallow of beer, discarded that can, and went toward the sound.

"Pssst! Pssssssst!"

"Pssssssssst!"

Tex found her sitting in the brush. "Hi," he said, kneeling beside her. He touched her hair and kissed her, then slipped his hand down the front of her dress.

"Let's hurry," she said, grabbing him around the neck and pulling him over on top of her. Tex ran his hand under her dress and discovered that she wore no panties. These country girls were as fast as the ones from the city.

"These damn ticks," she said, "are about to eat me alive."

They both giggled as Tex unbuckled his belt.

Applause filled the dance hall. People whooped, clapped, whistled, and stomped their feet, crying, "More! More!" Buck and Viv stood hugging each other, the song at an end. They parted and broke into the wilder strains of "Stay All Night."

The dancing began again. Kelly backed up against the wall; it was too fast for him. All the girls had just about worn him down. He had seen the good-looking one in the white dress go out the door and Tex follow her. He wondered how Jeannie could fail to understand what was going on between Tex and his women.

Rosella and Garland had cut loose, clapping and swinging around in the middle of the floor, dancing an improvised buck and wing. Garland looked like he was a little tight.

Some of the girls were dancing with each other, and Kelly took the opportunity to slip outside. He needed some air.

There was no sign of Tex and the girl. Kelly knew they had not climbed onto the bus, because he had watched it from the window; that meant they were down in the brush somewhere. Kelly bought a beer. He turned around to find Jeannie standing behind him.

"You ain't seen Tex, have you?"

Jeannie was a fine-looking woman. Kelly wondered if she was wearing the bra that Tex had given her as a present—the one with the holes in it.

"No," he told her, lying. He had a notion and added, "Wait a minute. I think I saw him walk over yonder toward the bus." Kelly had borrowed the bus from Buck to bring all their friends out from Austin; he knew Tex was nowhere near it.

"I'm gonna go look," Jeannie said.

"Here, lemme go with ya. I wouldn't want an old rattlesnake to jump up and bite you."

"Oh, Kelly." She smiled at him. "You're so sweet."

He smiled back. "Yeah, ain't I?"

Buck and Viv were singing another song now. The sound followed them into the darkness.

Jeannie paused outside the door of the bus. Kelly gave her a gentle nudge, and she stepped aboard. It was even darker inside, and all they could hear was the singing.

They walked to the back. Jeannie turned, and Kelly put his arms around her. She stiffened, but he kissed her anyway. Her arms slipped around his neck.

Kelly gently coaxed her down onto the seat. He unbuttoned her blouse and slipped his hand inside: it was the new bra, all right, holes and all.

Sid was tired of playing dominoes. He hadn't even had the opportunity to drink a respectable amount of beer, and the bartender was already passed out behind the bar. He saw Owen's wife peer down behind the beer stand. "Owen!" she wailed. "Ain't you ashamed!"

Sid matched up his last tile with Eubank's and took the old man's two dollars. He hoped he was finally broke.

"How about one more?" Eubanks said, producing more bills. He sounded desperate.

"You keep saying that."

Eubanks scowled at him. "You won't play me one more?"

"I want to dance," Sid said, "have some fun."

Eubanks stared at the stack of one-dollar bills in front of Sid. Suddenly he stood up, tipping the board. Dominoes and cash flooded into Sid's lap, and Eubanks stalked off into the darkness.

Sid began to patiently gather up his winnings. That was life, he thought: you had to put up with some humiliation if you were a winner.

Buck looked out over the crowd. He knew every single person in the hall, or so it seemed. That fact gave him more satisfaction than he could express. The evening made him a little melancholy, and the beer and good feelings made him talkative. "Well, folks," he said, into the mike, "this has been some kinda day, ain't it?"

They applauded, but there was less whistling now; the night was winding down.

"There's no place like home—that's for damned sure." Buck put his arm around Viv, to show how much he cared for her, and drew her close to him. "It sure is good to be with family. You all mean a lot to me, you really do."

This time the applause was long, and sincere. Buck and Viv looked at each other. They knew it was time for a change, for another kind of music.

"Come on up here, Jessie," he said. "Aunt Paula, you, too."

"Mary Lynn, come on now." Viv waved to some other women. "You, too, Lily."

They all had good voices. Jessie led the way, beaming at the call she had expected all night. She was known as a gospel singer, and she began to sing "Amazing Grace" in a rich, soulful voice.

> Amazing Grace, how sweet the sound
> That saved a wretch like me.

The other women stood in a group behind her, and they joined in, along with Buck.

> I once was lost but now I'm found,
> Was blind but now I see.

People on the dance floor began to sway. They put their arms around one another and opened their mouths to give expression to their deepest feelings.

> Grace that taught my heart to fear,
> And grace my fears relieved.
> How precious did that grace appear,
> The hour I first believed.

Buck took Viv's hand and led her down from the stage. The women and the crowd continued to sing. People smiled at them, they kissed Viv and patted Buck on the back as they made their way toward the door. Jamie sat sleeping in a chair by the open window, holding the bridle of his pony that stood outside. Buck gathered his son up in his arms. He and Viv went out and got the pony and started toward the parking lot.

Buck tethered the pony to the back of the

truck, and the three of them settled into the front seat. He started the motor without waking Jamie. Buck and Viv looked at one another. Then he put the truck in gear, and they drove slowly toward home, followed by the powerful sound of the chorus.

> I once was lost but now I'm found,
> Was blind but now I see.

8

Viv woke up at noon. It was as late as she had slept in a full year—since the day after the last Bonham reunion—and she lay for a moment looking out toward the pasture. She could hear Jamie talking to the pony in the yard and the measured breathing of Buck asleep beside her. She turned over and looked at him and softly touched his face. She wanted him to wake up and hold her, but then he needed his sleep. And sleep was the only thing that would keep Buck Bonham in one place for long; as soon as he woke up, he would be out with Jamie or jogging or hitting golf balls or on the telephone. His band was now one man short.

Viv had chores to do, like feeding her son. She sometimes wondered what Jamie thought about the change in their lives when Buck came home. She and Jamie kept regular hours when he was out on the road, but when daddy returned, they stayed up late and slept late and ate at funny times. It didn't seem to bother Jamie, however.

She got up and quietly went to the chair where her dress hung. She was about to step into it when she caught a glimpse of herself in the mirror. Her thighs and stomach were firm, she was still attractive, but probably not as attractive as some of the younger women who hung around Buck's bus.

"Damn, wish I had a woman like that."

She spun around and saw Buck watching her. He grinned, amused at having caught her examining herself. Viv was not a vain person.

"You do," she said, flattered. She had never belonged to anyone else.

"Don't think I've forgot."

She stepped into the dress, feeling oddly bashful in front of him. Buck could still get her rattled, after all these years.

"It was nice standing with you last night," he went on. "Just like old times."

"It really was." She slipped the straps over her shoulders and sat down on the edge of the bed to put on her shoes. "Felt real good," she admitted, although talking about performing made her uneasy. Viv was afraid Buck would ask her to go back out on the road.

"Viv?"

"What?"

"I don't have other women on the road."

They had never finished the conversation they began two days before. She turned and looked down at him, anxious to see if what he said was true. There were many things about Buck that remained unclear to her, which made him, in a way, more attractive to her. But she also worried.

"I mean," he said, "I have a few times, a long time ago. But I don't anymore."

Viv had always suspected that he had. That part of their relationship—the early days—didn't matter as much as the present.

"I don't know what to do," she said.

Buck seemed worried. "About what?"

"I know I'm being selfish. I know that, but every year you're on the road, it seems like ten, and I just want you all the time, so bad—" She paused, not wanting to sound too sentimental. But she

71

wanted Buck to know how she felt, and she had to tell him while she had the chance.

"I just want my arms around you," she said, "and around Jamie at the same time. All the time. I don't know what to do with all this love I have for you."

"Come back on the road with me." Things always seemed simple to Buck.

"We've already done that."

"Yeah," he said, "but this is too hard, being away from each other."

"That's true," she agreed.

"Well, come back out with me."

"I can't do that number." It was true. Times had changed, and Viv wanted her own life. "I can't get on that bus with a dozen guys and you, and stop at a different place every night—packing and unpacking every night. Besides, when we did it before, we didn't have a son. And anyhow, every time I ask you for a real answer, I get, 'Come back on the road.'" She felt a sudden unexpected rush of resentment. "Sometimes I feel like you don't want a family. You make all your efforts for strangers. None for us. You use Jamie and me like one of your audiences. You pop in, sing us a song, and then you're gone again."

She got up and walked to the window. "We're supposed to be glad you came through town," she added, her back to him.

"Well, hell," Buck said. "It's always suited you before."

"No, it never suited me." She turned and walked back to the bed and gripped the brass bedstead in both hands. "But you loved me, Buck. I thought one day you just might stay."

"I ain't doing this so I can retire someday. I like it! I like my life!"

"I don't wonder you like it. All you gotta do is remember the words to the songs." That was a little harsh, but she figured Buck could stand to hear it. "Nobody on the road ever asks more than that of you."

"That's right, they don't."

He kicked the sheet away and sat on the edge of the bed. He was mad, but Viv didn't care. It was time he faced a few facts, for his own good as much as for hers and Jamie's.

"What're you gonna do when all the music runs out, Buck? You think any of those people're gonna be there waiting for you?"

Buck glared at her. Then his expression softened, and he shook his head. "You know I can't quit."

"I never wanted you to quit. But, Buck, I want to ask you something. Is there ever going to be a time when you're really going to slow down?"

He didn't answer; he didn't have to.

"See what I mean?" she said.

She walked to the door.

"Where're you going?" he asked.

"I am going to get on the phone and get you a guitar player to take Garland's place."

She would let him think about that for a while.

Buck put on his jogging shorts and a pair of sneakers, and left the house without speaking to Viv. Garland's quitting was complicating every part of his life. Viv would not have been asking the questions if she hadn't had Garland's and Rosella's example to hold up to him. The fact was, Buck had not given a lot of thought to the future. Having to think about it as soon as he woke up and to deal with his wife's discontent took away some of the remembered pleasure from the night before.

73

Things had seemed perfect when they were singing together on the stage. In the hard light of day, he saw that she preferred to be at home.

He loped out across the meadow, toward the creek. The sun was hot, and Buck welcomed the feel of his own land beneath his feet. Pretty soon he was sweating, burning up all the Pearl beer he had drunk at the reunion.

He turned around at the bridge and started back toward the house. Jamie galloped toward him, waving and calling, "Papa!" He put the pony into a nice, smooth, sliding stop, as good as most any cutting or roping horse Buck had seen. He decided that he had gotten a deal on that pony and that Jamie was a better rider than anyone suspected.

"Fair set of brakes she's got," Buck said.

Jamie was proud of her, and of himself. "Reins good, too. Look it!"

Jamie dug his heels ino the little mare's flanks and put her through a quick figure-eight. He stopped her on a dime, swinging his leg over casually while her haunches were still lowered in the stop. Buck nodded in approval, smiling at his son's performance. Jamie seemed destined for the rodeo. He stood in a cowboy's stance, his feet wide-spread, and tipped the brim of his cowboy hat back with one finger. Buck had the feeling that Jamie, too, wanted to talk; he was acting like a grown-up.

"You been makin' good money out there on the road, papa?"

"Well, sure," Buck said, wary. "Pretty good, I guess."

"You been puttin' any of it away," Jamie wanted to know, "or you been blowin' it all on whiskey, and"—his composure faltered, for he wasn't sure what adults spent their money on—"things?" he added.

74

For a second Buck thought he was hearing his father talk, instead of his son. He cocked his head at Jamie, but the boy was dead serious. Buck decided to play along.

"What's the matter, you worrying about your college education or something?"

Jamie looked at the ground, hands in his pockets, considering his response. He took a step and with a practiced motion kicked a clod of dirt across the pasture. Then he confronted Buck again. "Whyn't you quit the road, come home, and raise some horses with me?"

So that was it. Buck couldn't believe he was getting it from both sides—mother and son. Worse, he knew that Viv would never put the boy up to it. Jamie had made his own plea. Buck could not take that lightly, and he couldn't argue with him, the way he could with Viv. His wife had married him for better or for worse, but Jamie had no choice.

"You been sayin' all along," Jamie continued, "that you was just out there making some money for a time when we could do something like that."

How could he explain to Jamie what it was like to perform, to write and play his own songs, to come up against a hallful of people in a different place every night who expected things of you, and deliver? He didn't have to explain it to Viv; she *knew*. But Jamie was just a kid. Buck wished he could make him understand, that he could make it all right.

All Buck could think of to say was, "Well, it's a little more'n money, Jamie."

He could see the determination drain out of the boy. He continued to swagger, but his heart wasn't in it now. "Yeah," he said, "I was afraid of that."

He tossed the reins over the pony's neck,

gripped the saddle horn, and threw himself into the rider's position. In another second he would have been gone.

"Hey, slick," Buck said, "wait a minute."

Jamie turned toward him. Buck grabbed his belt and gave him a friendly shake, bringing his face down close to Jamie's. He might have been angry, for all Jamie knew. Then Buck kissed him on the nose. Surprise and delight showed in Jamie's smile.

"Now don't tell 'em I did that," Buck said. "Wouldn't want it going around that Buck Bonham kisses cowboys on the nose."

Jamie rubbed his wet nose with the back of his hand. He seemed to forget that he was trying to appear grown-up. "Oh, papa," he said, with a touch of exasperation.

Buck turned, faced the house, and took a deep breath. "Come on. You want that horse to be in shape, she's gotta do her jogging every day."

They trotted side-by-side back to the ranch house. Then Jamie dug in his heels and galloped off toward the barn, waving his hat in one hand.

Buck went around to the little room behind the kitchen and opened the door. The room had once been a pantry, and a tack room before that, but Viv had converted it into an office, with file cabinets and a desk, and two telephones. She and Sid were each on one of the phones, trying to locate a replacement for Garland. Neither of them paid any attention to the sweaty leader of Buck Bonham's Band.

Viv hung up and said to no one in particular, "Longley signed with Buck Owens. We can't get him."

Buck had been counting on Longley. He was a name—and almost as good as Garland himself.

More than disappointment, Buck felt gratitude for Viv's efforts.

"You doin' any good?" she asked Sid.

He had a list in front of him on the desk, and he went down it with the point of his pencil. "Buddy Lewis ... Frank Dunn ... Bill Raby ... Berkley Edwards ... all committed somewhere. We can get a new boy, Cotton Roberts"—Sid checked his notes—"in three or four weeks."

"Sounds like a rabbit," Buck said. "Cotton Roberts." He had never heard the name.

"He's supposed to be good."

"What'll I do for three or four weeks? Go fishin'?" Buck couldn't wait for Cotton Roberts—or anyone else. "We got dates to play."

He sat down on the edge of the desk. The three of them thought for a while, but it was no good. They couldn't recruit any old guitar player.

Buck said, "Guess I'll figure some way to trick Garland into going back out." He could do it, if he had to.

"Don't try, Buck. Please." Viv was serious; she seemed to have forgotten their earlier discussion. "Rosella's given him an ultimatum. He leaves, she's going, too—in the other direction."

Buck wondered if there was a lesson there for him. He hated the organizational problems and anything that got in the way of a clean tour. Then he remembered one of the conversations he had found himself in the night before.

"I got a thought—it's off the wall—but it's only for three weeks. What about Lily?"

Sid looked from him to Viv. "Lily?"

"Garland's daughter," she said.

Sid liked the idea. "That's good show business."

"She's pretty good."

77

"No," Viv said. "That's dirty pool. Garland's come home to be with his family."

Buck had done enough for Garland. He wanted his friend to be happy, he wanted his friend's family to be happy, but Garland owed something to the band, too. "Garland should'a warned me before he hung up on me like this. It's only for three weeks."

"Yeah," Viv said, "it's only for three weeks."

Buck thought he heard a hint of sarcasm. He looked down into her big, velvety-brown eyes and knew he had heard right. There was something familiar about the phrase, something he had said years before. *It's only for three weeks.* They both knew that three weeks in the music business could turn into a lifetime, and usually did.

"Call him up," Buck said. There was an edge to his voice. Garland would have to make the decision.

Viv shrugged and picked up the telephone. She was a good soldier, to the end.

9

Coming into the Raw Deal Café off the sun-washed street, Buck had to pause and let his eyes adjust to the shadows. The place smelled of beer and cigarette smoke, pickled eggs, hamburgers and chicken-fried steaks sizzling on the grill, and a dozen other odors common to cafés and one-room bars all over Texas. The Raw Deal was old home week, everybody said so. Dolly Parton's voice was shaking the jukebox. Three regular old-timers sat at the end of the bar near the door so they could watch the traffic better, their elbows in beer suds and their scuffed boots tucked under the bar stools. Recognizing Buck, they all turned and offered him gap-toothed grins. The bartender gave him a wave. Behind the bar, above the battered cash register and the array of bottles, corn chips, and beef jerky in cellophane, hung posters advertising country music concerts in and around Austin, and others advertising the services of stud jackasses and stallions of good reputation.

Buck spotted Garland sitting in the back in a booth. His big felt hat hung on the peg. He sat staring at the steam rising from his coffee, and he didn't look up when Buck slipped onto the plank across from him. Garland had heard the proposition over the telephone and had agreed to discuss it, at least in principle. But Buck could tell from the looks of him that the answer was no.

Buck ordered coffee, too. He was willing to go along with Garland's mood—up to a point.

Finally he said, "It's only for a couple, three weeks."

"Four, you said."

Buck decided to let it mellow a little longer. He poured cream and then sugar into his coffee and raised the tarlike substance to his lips. The Raw Deal made coffee to last, that was for sure. Sometimes people drank whiskey just to get over the coffee.

"Well," Buck said, "then *you* come on back 'til this fella Cotton . . . What's-his-ass is free." It was the obvious solution, Rosella or no Rosella.

"I don't trust myself," admitted Garland. "If I go out, I might stay out. Rosella'd—"

He let it trail off. They both knew what Rosella would do, but that still left Buck without a guitar player.

"If she was a boy, you'd let her."

"Maybe—probably." Garland grudgingly nodded. "Sure. But I ain't certain I want my baby girl on that damn bus with those guys."

Buck understood the dilemma. He felt a little sorry for Garland, faced with it, but not too sorry. "She ain't much of a baby, Gar. Did you take a look at her lately?"

"Sure." Garland knew a pretty girl when he saw one. "That's what I mean."

Buck smiled and sipped his coffee. He wasn't going to push his friend any further.

Garland climbed the long flight of stairs leading to Lily's apartment above the drugstore. He had never been there before and wasn't sure he wanted to go now. Lily was a mystery to him. He had no one but himself to blame for that, and he had planned to get reacquainted. He still thought of her as she had been ten or twelve years before: a darling in pigtails. He hoped she still loved him, but he knew he couldn't count on that. Children didn't stand still, waiting for their fathers to come home. They had a way of their own of moving on, sometimes beyond reach.

He paused on the landing. The sound of a guitar being played slowly and meticulously seeped under the door, and Garland felt a rush of satisfaction. Lily could pick, all right. He had taught her himself, or at least got her started. Once his daughter had learned the basics, there had been no holding her back. But he was afraid that if she ever got on the music circuit, there would be no getting her off it. He had paid for her to go to college and study music, but it was a different sort of music—scholarly and respectable. Garland had always assumed she would end up teaching that kind of music, before she got married and started having children of her own.

That was the way he saw it. Now there was another possibility, one he had not figured on. He owed it to Lily to tell her about Buck's offer, but he also owed it to himself and Rosella—and to Lily— to discourage her from accepting it.

He knocked softly on her door. She answered wearing Levis and an old shirt with the top two buttons undone; she was barefoot. "Daddy!" She seemed pleased to see him, as well as surprised.

"Hello, baby."

"Come on in."

The apartment was bright and open. Garland could see the university tower through the front window; there were many students in the area, on the edge of the UT campus. Books were crammed into shelves at one end of the room, but the wall was decorated with posters of country music stars. He noticed that there were several photos of Buck among them.

"Want some coffee?"

"That'd be good," Garland said.

She went off to the kitchen, tossing her shoulder-length, dark brown hair out of her face, happy to serve her father. He sat in a spindly old rocker and surveyed the decor.

"You got a lot of my old friends up here," he called to her.

A door opened, and Garland thought it was Lily returning. He looked up and saw a young man standing between him and the bed, wearing nothing but a pair of Levis. His blond hair hung almost to his shoulders. He scratched his stomach, unperturbed by Garland's presence. "Mornin'," he said.

Garland was too surprised to speak. Otherwise, he might have gotten up and tossed the fellow down the stairs.

"Lily," the young man called, "you seen my blue shirt?"

She came in carrying two mugs of steaming coffee. "Daddy, this is Dorsey Lee. Dorsey, this is my daddy."

Dorsey smiled and stepped forward, extending his hand. "Good to meet you."

Garland shook it; he still didn't know what to say. All he could manage was a "Howdy."

"I sure admire your music," said Dorsey. Then he wandered to the bathroom.

Garland frowned at his daughter. He was more embarrassed than disapproving, intruding on Lily's private life.

"Oh, daddy," she said, amused at his reaction. She shoved a mug across the table.

"Well, goddamn, Lily." It was obvious that she

was living with Dorsey, or at least sharing some mighty intimate space with him.

"Daddy, I'm twenty-two—all growed-up and haired-over." It was an expression Garland had heard often enough, but he no longer liked it. He stood up, feeling he ought to leave.

"Lily, just listen to you talk."

She looked at him calmly, a smile still playing about the corners of her mouth. Garland realized then for the first time that she really was grown. He had seen plenty of girls her age—groupies who hung around the concerts and the clubs—who did what they pleased, whenever they pleased. But they weren't Garland's daughters.

"Come on, sit down," she said, gathering her feet up under her on the couch. "Drink your coffee."

Garland sat. When Rosella had told him where Lily was living, Garland had assumed she was just staying with a friend. A girlfriend. But this was Lily's apartment—furniture, roommate, and all.

"I was hoping," he said, "that you'd be living at home this summer."

"I just kind'a wanted my own place."

Garland tried to keep the disappointment from showing, but she quickly added, "I'll come visiting a lot, okay?"

"Yeah, all right." He sipped the coffee, uncomfortable with the place and with the news he carried. He decided he might as well get it over with. "Listen, Buck's thinkin' about asking you to go with 'em on the road awhile."

He saw immediately that she liked the idea.

"What'd you tell him?" Lily asked.

"It's just for a few weeks. After that, Cotton Roberts takes the job." Garland tried to make it sound as unattractive as possible. "You don't want to go on a little squirt like that, do you?"

83

"Yeah, I'd like to. I really would."

This time Garland didn't bother to conceal his feelings. He slumped down in the rocker. He had known she would say that, all along.

She leaned across the table and touched his hand. "I'm a musician, daddy."

"Aw, Lily, music's no kind'a life." He had to make her see that. "One-night stands, and it gets real rowdy on that bus. And in them motels . . ." It occurred to him that he was downgrading his own life. He was also talking about some aspects of being a musician that he had never brought up at home. "And parties, and drinkin'. You don't want the road."

"How do you know what I want?" She said it gently, but with more conviction than Garland could face. "You don't know anything about me, do you?"

He glanced toward the bathroom, where Dorsey was singing in the shower. She was right, but he still knew what was good for her, and what wasn't.

"No, maybe I don't," he admitted. "I'd like to, though. I'm home now."

"I been here my whole life, waiting. You took your own time getting here, didn't you?"

He could have cried then. He had not been afraid just of Lily accepting Buck's offer but also of her forcing him to look at himself as a father, as well as a musician. "I guess. . . ." There was nothing left to say, however. He wanted her to stay home so he could get to know her, he wanted her to get married and have children so Garland could start over again. He had missed the raising of his own. But then it was Lily's life to live, not his.

"I'm sorry, daddy, but this is my chance." She knelt beside him and put her hand on his knee. There was a hint of pleading in her voice that he

84

recognized from her childhood, when she had asked him not to go out on the road again. Now the roles were reversed. That was one big difference; the other was that Garland couldn't refuse her any more.

"Don't take it away from me," Lily told him. "I want to go."

10

Buck sat with his boots propped on the kitchen table, watching Jamie turn the crank on the old ice-cream maker. The slats of the wooden bucket were darkly streaked, and the mechanism groaned with each revolution. It was a tradition, making ice cream on the night before Buck went back out on the road. The box of rock salt had tipped over on the oil cloth, spilling the crystals, and an array of ice trays stood in puddles of water. Jamie had tossed blackberries into the bucket along with the cream and sugar, and his hands were stained purple.

Viv brought the enamel pot from the stove and poured Buck another cup of coffee. He patted her affectionately on the rump, and she touched his hair in passing.

Jamie panted, drooping with his hands on the crank.

"You need some more ice in there?" Buck asked. He added a shot of tequila to the coffee from a bottle of Sauza standing on the table.

"What we need is one of these with a motor on top. This is hard crankin'."

"Aw!" Buck teased. "When I was a kid, I had to churn butter for my mom. *That* was hard work."

But he got up and relieved Jamie. The crank was hard to turn. He dumped in the last of the ice and went to work.

Viv said, "Your mama told me you never did a lick a' anything but hide down by the creek pickin' a five-dollar guitar."

Jamie liked to hear Buck run down, as long as the criticism wasn't serious. He laughed and said, "I guess times haven't changed him much, huh, mom?"

"Out of the mouths of babes," said Viv. She kept her eyes on the turning handle.

Buck pretended to ignore the joshing. It was all part of the game. "This has gotta be finished." He unscrewed the top, and the three of them put their heads together and peered into the bucket. The thick, creamy, purplish ice cream clung to the blades.

"See!" said Jamie, grinning. "It's hard, isn't it?"

Buck nodded. Jamie lunged across the table and grabbed the big spoon. "Ooooh, boy! Lemme at it!"

Buck beat him to the draw. He thrust his finger directly into the ice cream and brought up a glob. He held it out to Viv, and she licked it from his finger.

"Mmmm," she said. There was nothing quite like homemade ice cream in July.

"Now wait, you guys," Jamie ordered. He lined up three bowls on the table. "We have to do this right." He handed his mother the spoon. "Dish it out."

Buck flicked his finger, thinking the excess ice cream would go back into the bucket. Instead, it hit Jamie's cheek. Jamie scraped it off and licked his finger clean. He dipped his finger into the bucket, Buck opened his mouth, and Jamie tried to flick the ice cream inside. But it landed on Buck's shirt.

In a moment the three of them were slinging ice cream into one another's faces, laughing and licking themselves clean. Buck loved the spontaneity of it, as did Jamie. Viv let it go on for a minute or two, then began to gently rap Buck's and Jamie's hands with the spoon. She portioned out most of what was left.

They carried their bowls into the living room and sat down on the floor. While they ate, they sang a silly little song about ponies and guitars and blackberry ice cream. Buck provided most of the words, and Jamie provided most of the laughter.

"That was a good one," he said. "Can I have some more ice cream?"

"You'll bust," said Viv.

Buck put his arm around his wife and pulled her to him. He kissed her in the ear, much to Jamie's delight. "Hit the sack, squirt," he told him. "Your mama and me're gonna go out and roll around in the wet grass."

"Buck!" She pulled away from him, pretending to be outraged. "Anyway, it's one o'clock in the morning."

Jamie was obviously pleased by their banter. But he stood up and collected the ice cream bowls with a child's quick officiousness. "Heck, mama," he said, and Buck recognized the tone of a grown-up cowboy that Jamie often used, "the grass ain't wet in the middle of the afternoon." Buck looked at Viv and laughed.

Jamie carried the bowls out to the kitchen. He came back and leaned over Buck, expecting a kiss.

"Night, daddy."

Buck put an arm around him, and the other around Viv, and pulled them both over on top of him. Jamie squealed with delight as the three of them rolled around on the rug in what sounded like a fierce embrace.

Then the three of them lay very still, and Buck almost wished that nothing would disturb that moment.

He woke up just before dawn. The music had done it—not a sound, but the beginnings of a new song. The words and the melody hummed in his head, trying to get out. He had to give them the chance, or he would feel restless all day. And Buck and the band had a long trip ahead of them.

He sat up and swung his bare feet to the cold floor.

"It's not mornin' yet," Viv said. Buck didn't know she was awake.

"I can't sleep."

He got up and began to dress. The windows glowed dully, but the hills beyond were still black.

"I've been thinking," he said. "We're back here for the Labor Day concert. Let's dedicate it to Garland this year. Make the whole thing for him." Buck felt some guilt about Lily; she had chosen the road over her father. At least that was the way Garland saw it.

"That's good," Viv said. "He'd like that a lot."

Buck sensed that there was more. He couldn't see her in the darkness, just the outline of her blond hair. He knew his leaving tore her up.

"Listen," he began, not knowing exactly what he was about to say, "maybe I'll take some time off after the Labor Day thing. How would that suit you?"

"I'd love it," she said simply. But Viv wasn't convinced that he was serious.

"No, I mean it. You ever think about that?" It annoyed Buck that she didn't believe him.

89

"Sure," Viv said softly, "every time you say it, you mean it." She paused, then added, "Buck, don't say anything to Jamie about takin' some time off."

"Why not?"

" 'Cause he'll believe it."

Buck didn't argue. Viv knew him better than he knew himself—he had no intention of slowing down, at least not yet. That didn't mean that he was indifferent to his family's welfare or their happiness.

"I do love ya'll, Viv."

"I know you do. I love you, too."

He slipped on his down vest and snapped it shut. He picked up his guitar. "I'll be down at the creek."

"The bus leaves at ten," she reminded him.

Buck nodded. He passed silently through the house so as not to wake Jamie and stepped out onto the front porch. Dawn had broken. The air was cool and smelled of the dew. Buck carried the guitar across the yard, past the gate, and through the meadow toward the creek. The big cottonwood trees formed massive shadows in the early light. The bullfrogs croaked on, unwilling to give up the darkness.

A bench had been built between two of the cottonwoods years before. Buck sat there, crossed his legs, and strummed the guitar once. The sound blended easily with the morning. He paused, trying to remember the melody that had wakened him, the excitement, and the sense of loss that were part of the same song. He began to play a tight, slurred, dissonant passage. The words of the song dealt with his life on the road, how he had to keep going and how difficult that was for others to understand. He tried to fit them to the music, and he let the music inspire new words. Often he stopped to play the first passage again, like a refrain.

Buck didn't know how long he had been sitting on the bench. When he looked up, he saw light touching the tops of the hills to the west and Jamie standing directly in front of him. The boy wore only pajamas and a pair of cowboy boots.

"Hey, punkin," Buck said, "what're you doin' down here?"

"I heard you from up at the house." Jamie looked scared. "You all right?"

"Oh, yeah, just sittin' here."

Buck motioned Jamie down onto the bench beside him. They sat looking out over the dammed-up creek, toward the far pasture. Buck felt a rush of affection.

"You hear that?" he asked Jamie.

"Those frogs croakin'?"

"In between the croaks. Listen."

They both listened. Buck pretended he heard something.

"I don't hear nothin'," Jamie said.

Buck strummed his guitar, and began to sing.

"Oh, papa." Jamie laughed, realizing he had been fooled. Buck laughed with him.

"My daddy taught me that one."

"Know any more?"

Buck tried to think. But he felt Jamie trembling beside him.

"Hey, slick, you're shivering."

He got up and made Jamie put on his down vest. Then he hung the guitar over Jamie's shoulder. They wrapped their arms around each other and headed back to the house.

The band members began to arrive after breakfast. Within half an hour the road was jammed with cars and pickups belonging to family and friends. Luggage, instrument cases, and sound equipment sat in the grass or on top of the bus .

where Rooster crouched, tying each piece down. People kissed and hugged, their laughter quick but shortlived. In a few minutes they would all be scattered again.

Buck waited for the other musicians to file onto the bus. He was expecting Jamie, and when he rode up on the pony, Buck put his arms around his neck and hugged him tightly.

"Don't get saddle sore," he said.

"I love you, daddy."

"Oh, boy, me too. And then some."

They both smiled bravely. Jamie wanted to cry, but Buck knew he wouldn't let himself.

Viv stood off to one side, watching them, and Buck winked.

Sid walked up to her. He stuck out his hand, and Viv shook it absently.

"Keep in touch," she said. "I want to know how it goes."

"All right. You'll send Cotton Roberts along to catch up with us?"

"Yeah."

Buck turned and put his arms around Viv's waist. "Sid, I been thinking about dedicating the Labor Day concert to Garland this year. Make the whole thing for him."

"Good idea."

"Tell him, will ya. I need to talk to this woman."

Garland and Rosella both had their arms around Lily. "Bye, honey," Rosella was saying. "Don't forget to come back." If it was a joke, nobody laughed.

"We'll take care of her," Sid said.

Garland gave his daughter one last hug. "Well, play good, baby."

"I will, daddy. 'Bye, mama."

Buck could tell that Lily was anxious to get out of view. She almost skipped onto the bus.

"Garland, Rosella," Sid said, "Buck wants to know if you'd be embarrassed if we were to throw the Labor Day concert in your honor."

Buck looked away before Garland could catch his eye. He knew Garland would be flattered; he didn't want it to seem like compensation for losing Lily for four weeks.

"Why don't you just show up some night," Buck whispered to Viv. "You 'n Jamie."

"Where?"

"Anywhere. Tulsa, maybe." He shrugged. "Surprise me."

That brought the light back to her eyes. "Oh, Buck." She gave him a full, passionate kiss.

"See you, kiddo," he said, releasing her. He picked up his guitar case. Before he could board the bus, Garland stepped forward and gripped his arm. "Sid told me what yer planning for Labor Day. I like that."

"I like you, too, Garland." Buck had to tell him, even though it choked Buck up for a second. He had never felt quite like this when leaving Viv and Jamie, and then for the first time he was hitting the road without his oldest buddy. Buck was surprised by the emotion he felt, but he made no attempt to hide it. "Yep," he added, hitting Garland lightly on the arm, "they ought'a make a statue out'a you, hoss."

Garland blinked furiously, keeping back the tears. "If they ever do," he said, "I want'a be mounted on my new John Deere, plowin'. That's what I'm gonna be up to from now on out."

Buck shook his head in disbelief. "If you're a farmer, Gar," he said, swinging aboard, "then I'm a brain surgeon."

93

The motor started with a shudder. Rooster, in the driver's seat, wheeled the bus through a big U-turn and headed up the road toward the highway.

Buck leaned out the open door and shouted, "See ya Labor Day!" Everyone waved and shouted, on the bus and off. A cloud of dust rose to separate them, along with the distance. The last thing Buck saw was Jamie in pursuit on his pony, his cowboy hat raised in farewell.

11

I just can't wait to get on the road again.
The life I love is making music with my friends,
And happiness is on the road again.

For as long as Lily could remember, she had
wanted to travel with a band. Long before playing
the guitar became second nature to her, before she
could read music or even remember the words to
the songs that filled the Ramsey house, she felt the
pull of the road. A concert tour was a strange,
glorious journey that drew her father away from
home time and time again; it had to be glorious,
and irresistible, or how else could he have left Lily,
her brothers and their mother on the farm, to do so
many of the chores meant for a man? Later, after
she realized that touring was just what her father
did for a living, a job like driving a truck · or
teaching school, the road lost none of its attraction.
Music was made on the road, and reputations. The
road led up and out if you were good, and Lily had
known for a long time that she was good. A strong
sense of independence was one thing you developed if you were the daughter of a popular musician; a critical ear was another.

Garland was her father, and a name in country
music, but Buck was her idol. For ten years she
had been acutely aware of the sound of his voice,

the lyrics that he wrote, and of him as a presence in her life. She had changed a great deal, but he had remained constant. His voice had an ethereal quality that interested her, and his songs spoke to her in a special way—songs about hard times, about personal suffering and the need to be yourself and about the unpredictability of love. The more Lily had learned in college about the structure and the history of music, the more she realized how unique Buck was.

Now Lily was on the road, and she was to perform with Buck Bonham, and she still couldn't believe it. She had always thought of him as a distant, radiant star, even when he came to her house, warm and friendly but beyond her touch. Now he sat ten feet away from her on the same bus, slumped in his seat, writing lyrics with a pencil on a long yellow pad. He looked up and gave her that sad smile, and Lily had to look away, so strong was the emotion she felt.

The band members all sat around the poker table, with the exception of Bonnie, who bent over her needlepoint, an island of calm in the middle of loud and persistent banter. Lily watched Sid lay down a winning hand and rake in a large pot while the others hooted and groaned. Sid wore a hat with the broadest brim she had ever seen and a leather band with a turkey feather in it. Lily thought it was the sort of hat a business manager might wear. Sid had bought it, he had boasted, with the money he had won off old man Eubanks at the Bonham family reunion.

"That's a new hat, ain't it, Sid?" Kelly asked, although he already knew the answer.

"Yeah," Sid said proudly, running a hand along the brim—a foot out from his head. "You like it?"

Kelly nodded. "It's a good one, ain't it?" Then he burst out laughing. Kelly played the harmonica like a dream, Lily thought, and he was the musician closest to her in age. She liked the way he dealt with the older men—as equals.

"It's just amazing," Bo said, shuffling the cards, "what they can do nowadays with cow flop."

"Deal, asshole." Sid pretended he wasn't insulted. "I might wanna buy another one."

"Anybody here got a college education?" Bo asked innocently.

"Yeah," Lily said, "I do."

"Run back there and get me a beer, then, will you? We don't want nobody's education goin' to waste."

She had to laugh with the others. She didn't care that the bass player had bested her—at least she was being noticed, officially. They had all taken stock of her female charms when she stepped on the bus, but that wasn't the same thing.

She walked back past Buck to the refrigerator.

"I could use one, too," Bliss called.

"Me, too," said Jonas.

"Better just bring an armful," suggested Sid.

Lily took out a six-pack. She started to ask Buck if he wanted a beer but then thought better of it. She didn't want to seem like she was forcing herself on him.

She carried the beer forward. "Here you go," she said cheerfully, handing the cans around. She noticed the little video camera attached to the ceiling and the monitor the band used for rehearsing. She saw a way to get back at Bo for his little joke about her college education.

"Thanks," Bo said, when she gave him his Pearl. "That college education comes in real handy, don't it?"

Lily smiled sweetly. As she did so, she reached behind him and flipped the switch on the monitor.

His poker hand appeared on the screen, visible to everyone but Bo. They all smiled, but no one gave the joke away.

Bliss said, "Your bet, Bo."

"I'm bettin' ten dollars." Bo slapped the money down on the table. He had aces and sixes, and he was proud of it.

"Hmmm," Bliss said, pretending to consider his hand. "Well, I'm seein' "—he drew the word out, and repeated it—"seein' ya. And I'll raise you twenty."

Bo hesitated and then tossed in his twenty dollars. The others could barely stifle their laughter, except for Tex. He was staring at something under one of the seats. His smile faded, replaced by a frown of such intensity that Lily was afraid he had found a body. Tex went down on his hands and knees. When he came up again, he held between his thumb and forefinger a lacy bra decorated with red ribbons and with holes in the middle of the cups.

Tex threw the bra down onto the table, knocking over Bo's beer.

"You're bettin' out of turn," Bo said calmly, picking up and shaking his money dry. "And look what you've done to my beer."

"I wanna know how that got on this bus," Tex said, pointing at the bra. He was furious, but Lily couldn't figure out why.

"Looks like Rooster's," said Sid with a straight face. Everyone stared at it.

"Bullshit!" Tex shouted. "I wanna know how it got on this bus. One of you guys has been foolin' with my girl."

The laughter dried up. Tex was a big man, with forearms like a bull rider's, and a drummer's natural meanness. The band members all exchanged glances.

"I'm waitin', by God," Tex said.

Someone had to confess. Otherwise, Tex would suspect everyone, and that would mean bad blood for the rest of the tour. Lily could see how such a seemingly trivial incident could have very serious consequences.

The others instinctively understood, too. Finally Kelly whispered, "It was me, Tex."

"Why, you bastard." Tex turned toward him, his fists clenched. Kelly looked very frail in comparison, with his long, thin neck and his reddish curly hair in his face. Lily was afraid Tex would hit him, but then she heard Jonas say, "I admit it. I took a turn with her myself."

Tex's mouth fell open. "Why you son of a—"

"Yeah, I did, too," Bo said.

"Me, too," Bliss added. He jerked his thumb toward the front of the bus. "But old Rooster was first. We had to pry him off with a crowbar."

Tex turned from one to the other, his face bright pink, his knuckles white. Everyone began to laugh at once. Tex would have to fight them all if he was going to fight one; a little lovemaking wasn't worth all that aggravation. It was a well known fact that Tex had more girls than anybody, even Kelly.

Cursing to himself, he sat back down and picked up his soggy poker hand.

"Get me another one, honey," Bo said, mopping up his spilled beer with a red bandanna.

"Hey, Bo," Buck called from the back of the bus, "she was signed on to pick, not to serve you."

Lily didn't mind. She brought Bo another Pearl and then went back and sat down across the aisle from Buck. She was pleased that he was looking out for her.

"Don't pay any attention to them," he said.

"Their spirits are always kinda high when we go back on the road again."

"I guess they're not used to having a young woman on the bus."

Buck looked at her as if she were crazy.

"I mean a musician," she quickly added. Bonnie didn't really qualify as a *young* woman.

"Yeah," Buck said, laughing in that quiet way he had, "they never treated Garland like that."

"What was my daddy like on the road?" She could not imagine him playing poker all the time with the boys, making jokes and chasing girls.

"Garland, he was in it for the music." Buck looked down at the words scribbled on the sheet in his lap and then out at the passing country. "Never fooled around much or nothing. He was a damn fine daddy to you, I can tell you that."

Lily was pleased that Buck took up for her father, whether or not what he said was true. She felt a rush of exhilaration. She was on the road, she was doing what she had always wanted to do, and nothing else mattered. She wanted Buck to feel that special high, too.

"How many miles does it take you, Buck?"

"For what?"

"To get over feeling guilty and sad"—Lily hoped she wasn't crowding him—"at leaving people behind."

"What makes you think I'm feeling guilty and sad?"

It was obvious, at least to her. "Well, ain't ya?"

"It shows, huh?" Buck was still counting fence posts. "You know, I do love them." He turned and looked directly at her, wanting something settled. "Don't hold it against Garland—him being gone all the time."

Lily knew he was talking about himself as

much as he was about Garland. She figured she knew as much about Buck as he knew about himself, and maybe more. And right then he wanted someone to understand the pull of the road and even forgive him for following it.

"Don't assume I hate my daddy," she told him, "just 'cause he was seldom home."

"I didn't. I just—"

"Garland and I've always been closer than he thinks we have. I missed him, sure, but"—she thought about what it was like, all those years; it had not been so bad—"I'd just listen to his music and figure he was out cuttin' a path for me to follow in the world."

Buck turned in his seat to get a better look at her. That made Lily uneasy.

"You're pretty ambitious, ain't you?"

The judgment disappointed her. It had to be more than that.

"It's not ambition," she said. "Is it? I mean, I love music, and I want to be good at it. Just like you."

She saw the affection in Buck's smile. She rested her head against the back of the seat and closed her eyes.

"I don't believe," she happily announced, "I'm on this bus!"

She stood in the dark, gripping her guitar, running her fingers up and down the frets. She had a terrible, empty feeling in the pit of her stomach, and her hands shook. Every time she glanced beyond the heavy folds of the curtain bunched at the side of the stage, she saw a thousand faces half-hidden in the gloom of the hall, a sea of hats, Levis and plaid shirts, ties, eyeglasses, teeth and glints of light off the occasional upturned bottle. She could hear the waves of that sea breaking against the walls, restless, expectant. She could smell marijuana and cigarette smoke and the smoldering spots above the stage, trained on Tex's drum set and the microphone stands that sprouted from the boards like petalless flowers.

She was boxed in by the other band members, all waiting for the show to begin. They all seemed relaxed, happy, oblivious to the terror the crowd held for her. The exhilaration she had felt on the bus had evaporated when the spotlights came on. She had overrated her ability; she was never going to make it as a professional musician, and it was just a matter of minutes before the whole world knew.

She tried once more to tune the instrument she knew so well. It refused to respond. Her hands were made of wood.

She whispered, "Damn."

"Nervous, Lil?" It was Buck. He wore a beaded headband to keep the now unbraided hair out of his face. He put his arm around her, and Lily thought she would drop on the spot.

"Somethin' fierce," she admitted.

"Nothin' to it, kid." He smiled down at her, the blues he had felt on the bus forgotten. That helped her. She could feel his eagerness to perform. "We just throw it out there and see what they throw back."

Sid motioned them forward. It was almost time.

"Hey, Sid," Buck said, "mind if I wear that hat tonight?"

Sid was pleased. "You bet." He swept the big hat off and handed it to Buck. The wide brim dwarfed him. Buck looked around to see if the others liked the hat and then without warning marched out onto the stage. Lily was pushed forward in front of Bo and Bliss, into the spotlights. The crowd roared, and she felt an enormous rush of adrenalin. She was really on stage with the Buck Bonham Band. Buck struck a chord, and they all began to play—Lily included—a thundering version of "Whiskey River" that brought the audience to its feet.

> Whiskey River take my mind;
> Don't let her memory torture me.
> Whiskey River don't run dry.
> You're all I've got, take care of me.

Something happened to Lily. The fear was gone, but so was the exhilaration. Her fingers moved like lightning, her voice was clear and strong. She felt a sense of purpose new to her, a realization that what she was doing at that moment was real, perfect, lasting. The purity of that emotion overwhelmed her, joyous, sexual in intensity. Every care and every anxiety faded into insignificance, and she threw herself utterly into the music.

Then they segued into "Good-Hearted Woman." The transition was effortless, the applause blending with the music.

> A long time forgotten are dreams
> That just fell by the way.
> And the good life he promised
> Ain't what she's living today.

People crowded around the stage, many of them offering their hats to Buck in exchange for his wide-brimmed Stetson. To Lily's amazement, Buck took off the hat and sailed it out over the heads of his fans. Another hat came sailing back. It was old and misshapen, with a tiny brim and no feather. Buck picked it up and put it on. Whistles and shouts filled the hall.

Lily noticed that Sid, in the wings, stared out at the crowd in disbelief, while Rooster was doubled over with laughter.

You need a sense of humor, she thought, to belong to this group.

She didn't miss a chord.

The concert was over before she knew it. She was patted and congratulated, and people climbed up on the stage to meet Garland Ramsey's daughter. Lily could have gone on singing and picking forever, but there was not even time for a party. They had to be in Oklahoma City the next day, and as soon as Rooster had the equipment packed and loaded, they all filed onto the bus.

Buck was driving. Lily hoped he would ask her to sit in the seat next to him, but he didn't. She went to the back and curled up on her own seat. As soon as the bus began to roll, she closed her eyes on what had been the best day of her entire life. Instantly she fell asleep.

12

The huge amphitheater filled with the sound of cheering. Lily looked up into the high bank of lights and saw smoke swirling there like clouds across the moon. The night throbbed with the music and the response of the fans. What they were throwing back, she realized, was love. Love for the sound and love for the words, love for the moment and for the musicians, but mostly it was love for Buck. He wore the old hat he had retrieved from the stage the night before, his pigtails whipping as he led them deeper into the song. His voice cut through the roar, clean and vibrant, while he watched the action in the wings.

Lily looked over and saw Emmylou Harris standing behind the curtain, beaming out at Buck. She wore boots and a long peasant-style dress, and her hair was tied up in a knotted scarf. As Lily watched, Emmylou detached herself from the tight knot of her friends and, responding to Buck's song, stepped onto the stage. At first the audience did not recognize her. Then the whistles and applause swelled as she crossed toward the band, arms outstretched, head thrown back. She needed no introduction.

She took the microphone, and a hush fell over the hall. She sang the next lines of the song to Buck.

We come here quite often and listen to
    music,
Partaking of yesterday's wine.

She and Buck sang together, their faces inches
apart, the strength of their friendship coming
through the music.

    Yesterday's wine, well, yesterday's wine
    Aging with time, like yesterday's wine.

Lily couldn't believe it. She was performing
with Buck Bonham *and* Emmylou Harris, two of
the biggest names in country music. Lily was en-
thralled by the sound of their mingled voices, the
sincerity of their emotion, the way the crowd
roared its approval as Emmylou stood back and
Buck came in with the next verse.

Suddenly someone was hissing at her. "Hey,
Lily," said Tex in an urgent whisper. She looked
back and saw the drummer grinning, pointing at
her guitar. She looked down and realized that she
had forgotten to play.

She began to pick furiously, the blood rushing
to her cheeks.

The suite at the Holiday Inn resounded with
laughter and the shouts of a stoned Rooster as he
resisted a golf lesson. Bo had him standing in the
middle of the floor, fitting a headband to him,
while the other band members and the local crowd
looked on. Rooster's eyes were glazed, and he
grinned at everyone who passed, but mostly he
grinned at the girls. They were young and some of
them quite beautiful, and they seemed available to
most any of the men, as long as those men played
guitar or harmonica or one of the pieces in Buck's
band, or had some intimate connection with it.

"Now bend down a little, Rooster," Bo was saying. "Take your natural stance."

Rooster pretended that he held a golf club in his hands. Standing with his feet spread apart on the rug where beer and cigarette ashes had been spilled, he stared down at an imaginary golf ball. Bo tied a cord to the headband compressing his glossy black hair, and he attached the hook of a coat hanger to the end of the cord. This he attached to the crotch of Rooster's trousers.

"Okay," Bo announced, "this device is gonna teach you to keep your head down. Go on, take a swing. You'll see how it works."

Rooster drew up his hands, as if to swing. The cord drew tight, hiking up the trousers. "Screw you, man!" he shouted at Bo. "I ain't gonna pull my *cojones* off!"

Rooster's complaint was drowned in more laughter. The crowd shifted, constantly moving, fed by a steady stream of loyal fans and locals drawn to the motel by the promise of a party and the stellar light of the band. Lily, her back in a corner, wasn't sure exactly where she fit into the scene. She was taking it slow, drawing on the good feeling about her and the sweetish smell of marijuana. The smoke was so thick in the room she didn't even need a toke. People drank beer or wine out of plastic cups, pressing in at the door, necks craned for a glimpse of Buck or Emmylou—or maybe even Garland Ramsey—working their way along the walls, toward the action. Bo, Tex, Kelly, and the others seemed adept at handling the adulation, joking and cavorting with friends or strangers. Lily wasn't sure she could do that; she wanted to get close to Buck, on the far side of the room.

Sid sat on the couch, and he looked up at her and winked. He wore the battered old hat Buck had brought from Amarillo as a substitute for the new one. Lily wasn't sure what he meant by the wink, and she didn't really care. The sexual currents in the room were very strong but unthreatening, friendly, mellow.

A groupie in a see-through blouse and a turquoise choker sat down next to Sid. "You like me?" she asked, throwing back her shoulders.

"I like you so much I'm giving you this hat so you'll remember how much fun we've had together."

He took it off and set it at an angle on her head. Lily supposed that the girl had already been to Sid's room with him, but she couldn't be sure. Sid was too cool to let it show.

"God, thanks—"

"Sid," he corrected.

"Yeah," she said, remembering, "Sid."

Lily was impressed by the girl's gratitude for an old hat. She got up and swayed through the crowd, showing off her acquisition.

Lily wasn't immune to the celebration. People kept coming over to congratulate her on her playing, which meant more to her than the fact that she was Garland's daughter. That, too, got the strangers excited. They liked the tradition of guitar playing in the Ramsey family, and Lily had to admit she liked it, had counted on it, in fact. Women patted her on the back, and the men shook her hand, and soon she had been pried out of her corner by her new admirers. All the attention was confusing, but she had to admit it was just as exciting.

Someone pressed a glass of wine into her hand. A girl held up a joint, and Lily took a drag of the Acapulco gold. She saw that Buck was watching her and smiling encouragingly, although he was hemmed in by the fans. They seemed to worship him. Lily had expected enthusiasm, but not adulation. She began to see why her father had stayed on the road so long and how difficult it must have been for him to give it up.

Buck waved to her, and Lily waved back and silently toasted him with the wine. She had always known he was great, had listened to his music and rated him above Johnny Cash, George Jones, Waylon Jennings and a bevy of other country singers, but she had never before this trip come into direct contact with Buck's talent. It was stronger and more vital than she had suspected, and suddenly essential. Lily couldn't imagine not being able to make music with him. She realized that she was as starry-eyed as the women now crowded around him—one of whom was holding up a baby for Buck's inspection—but there was nothing she could do about it.

Bonnie sat on a couch drinking a Pearl and watching the action. Lily pushed her way past elbows and hips and sat down beside her. She was attracted by Bonnie's calm sense of purpose and her good humor. Bonnie was also the only other woman in the band, and therefore a natural ally.

"How's it goin'?" Bonnie asked, taking Lily's hand.

"Okay, I guess." Lily let out a big sigh. "Pretty heady stuff, Bonnie."

"Yeah, they like us, don't they?"

"They seem to like Buck the most."

Lily couldn't keep her eyes off him; he seemed to genuinely like the people and the life.

Bonnie was bound to notice. "Buck's nice, ain't he?"

"He sure is," Lily admitted.

"Don't fight it, honey."

Lily looked at her closely. She recognized the voice of hill-country wisdom and fatalism.

"Plenty of women have fallen for Buck," Bonnie said, patting her hand, "and plenty of 'em will again. Just remember that gettin' in love's not nearly so troublesome as gettin' out of it."

13

Buck watched the last couple stumble out of
the room. It was Tex and the girl in the battered
hat, holding him up with both arms around his
thick mid-section, looking up at him with doubtful
eyes. Every table was covered with empty glasses,
many full of cigarette butts doused in the last of
the wine. The wastebaskets brimmed with empty
beer cans. Someone had written Go For It on the
mirror with lipstick, and the radio seeped all-night
country music into the room, broadcast from some
desolate outpost beyond the city limits. A typical
post-concert disaster scene.

He fell backwards into a chair. He was a little
high from the beer and the pot but far from wast-
ed. He didn't want the party to end. He wouldn't
be able to sleep until after dawn, still a couple of
hours away.

Sid sat stretched out on the couch, the only
other survivor. "You ready to fold?" he asked,
planting a fist in the middle of a yawn.

"Let's talk awhile."

"What about?"

What a question, Buck thought. He just
wanted some companionship, someone to shoot the
breeze with. "Hell, I don't care—volcanoes, earthquakes, horse trailers. . . ." Sid didn't pick up on
any of those subjects. "Pick something."

111

"Bed," Sid said. "Sleep, nocturnal bliss." He swung his feet to the floor. "We've got a lot of miles tomorrow, Buck."

Buck looked around. There was nothing worse than a motel room after a good party. "Goddamn, where's Garland? He knows a lot about volcanoes." This time of night, Garland was always the best company.

Sid heaved himself to his feet. Buck's stamina always impressed and amused Sid. "See you in the morning," he said, clapping Buck on the shoulder.

"Yeah." Buck didn't want him to leave, even if he didn't know anything about volcanoes. "See you in the morning."

Sid went out. Buck switched on the television set and sat for a minute looking at an old black-and-white western. He had seen it fifty times already, and besides, the sound didn't work on that channel. He twirled the selector but had worse luck elsewhere. All he saw were patterns on the screen.

He got up and opened the door onto the corridor. Tex and the girl still hadn't located Tex's room. Buck heard the girl ask him, "You gonna let me stay all night?"

"We'll have to see about that, darlin'."

Buck watched him try to fit his key into Rooster's door. From inside the room came a blood-curdling scream, followed by a stream of obscenity—in Spanish.

Tex was unperturbed. "Yeah," he drawled, "I'd say the gal old Rooster's got in there is just about average, wouldn't you?"

The groupie looked less confident. She pulled the hat down around her ears, and the pair of them moved to the next door.

"What the hell was that?" Buck asked. He

figured Rooster was just playing a joke, but the scream was mighty convincing.

Sid had also come out into the corridor—in his underwear. "It sounded like Rooster."

Buck walked up and knocked on the door. "You okay?" he called.

"Yeah, amigo," Rooster answered. His cursing tapered off, the intrusion forgotten.

"Come on," Buck urged Sid, "let's go get a drink."

"Buck"—Sid looked down at his bare legs— "I'm exhausted. I gotta lot of work to do tomorrow."

He shrugged and went back into his room, leaving Buck alone in the hallway. He stood there trying to decide whether or not to have a drink by himself. He heard music. At first he thought the guitar picking was coming from his radio, but then he realized that it was live, that someone was practicing.

He moved from door to door, listening. Finally he knocked. "Jonas?" He had never known Jonas to be so conscientious.

The music stopped. The door opened, and he found himself looking down at Lily. Her headband was gone, and her dark hair had been brushed smooth down to her shoulders.

"Oh," Buck said, feeling foolish, "I thought it was Jonas."

"Do you need something?" Lily seemed as fresh as she had at the beginning of the concert. He wondered if she had inherited her father's conversational talent along with his musical talent.

"Do you know anything about volcanoes?"

Lily smiled at him. "Volcanoes?"

"Me and your daddy used to sit around talking about such stuff in places like this."

She stepped back, opening the door wide.

113

"Come on in. I can't sleep, anyway. Still on cloud nine, I guess."

Buck liked her enthusiasm, but it bothered him, too. "Well," he said, "don't get to likin' it all too much." He followed her into the room. Her guitar lay on the bed; she had already packed for the trip out in the morning. "Or we'll never get you back to finishing college—"

"Buck," she laughed, interrupting him. She gave him the look he remembered from the day of the Bonham reunion, when she had called him a hypocrite. "I guess I gave up all thought of finishing college," she said, "on the second chorus of 'Whiskey River' our first night on stage."

"Oh, boy, now I really am in trouble with your daddy."

He sat heavily in a chair and propped his boots on the bed. He was counting on Lily changing her mind again and going back to school. For Garland's sake.

"And don't forget," he added, "you're only on this tour for a coupl'a, three weeks."

"Don't remind me."

"That *was* the deal." Buck didn't want any misunderstanding on that score. Lily was temporary, good as she was in concert.

She smiled, showing she was not ungrateful. "Well, three weeks in paradise is better'n nothin' at all."

Buck looked around, at the washable wallpaper, the identical carpeting, the phony veneer on the dresser, and the mass-produced artwork in the plastic frame. "Pretty funny-lookin' paradise," he said.

Lily sat down on the bed, next to his feet. She clasped her hands and leaned forward, her elbows resting on her thighs, her face close enough to his

114

for him to see the different shades of brown in her eyes.

"I mean, it's paradise just not having to think about anything else, not even noticing the rest of the world exists outside of the songs."

Buck had always felt that way. Few people could understand it, although Lily seemed to instinctively. He admitted to himself what he had known all along, that she was hooked on music and the road, and nothing he or Garland could do would change her mind.

"Yeah," he said. It was a kind of paradise.

"And, of course"—she didn't avert her gaze, a smile playing about the corners of her mouth—"being with you."

Buck wasn't prepared for that. Girls sitting on beds in motels at four o'clock in the morning were tempting, and common enough, even when they weren't as pretty as Lily. But Lily was different. Physically she awakened a desire in him that he managed to suppress when he was on the road, but she also talked about things that mattered most to him. The combination made him uneasy, occurring as it did in his best friend's daughter.

Lily sensed his discomfort. She dug into the pocket of her shirt and produced a tightly rolled joint.

"Wanna burn one now?"

Buck frowned. He smoked marijuana himself, but he didn't approve of it for Lily. He wasn't sure she could handle it.

"Where'd you get that?" he asked, as if it weren't easy to score off the people who hung around the band. Or off the band members themselves. He was beginning to wish that he had left Lily in Austin.

"At the party," she said. "It's probably one of yours."

"You better slow down, kid, 'fore you get us both tarred and feathered."

"If I only have a couple weeks out here," she told him, "I don't have time to slow down."

Buck stood up and walked to the window. Lily didn't believe in holding back. He would have to distract her.

He swept the curtain aside, revealing black sky beyond the window. "What time is it?"

"Not too far from morning."

"How 'bout some breakfast?" Buck suggested.

The diner was almost empty. It smelled of hot grease and cheap coffee brewed in a big stainless-steel urn next to the grill. Pies stacked in a glass case at the end of the counter looked like they had been there for the lifetime of the place, although the scrambled eggs and sausage Buck had ordered were worth the money. The scene reminded him of his early days on the road. A drunk in a torn shirt slumped on one of the stools, ignoring his hamburger, occasionally raising his head to stare glassy-eyed at the cook and begin another rambling account of the previous night's activities. The cook ignored him, his greasy apron pressed against the chopping board while he turned the pages of the morning newspaper. A truck driver sat a few stools down from the drunk, meditating on his steaming coffee, collecting himself before rolling off another few hundred miles. His semi was one of several trucks lining the roadside, the other drivers asleep in their curtained bunks behind the seats.

Maybe it was the diner, or Lily's prompting, or just the fact that it was dawn, but Buck began his own rambling account of his life. The more he talked, the more he remembered. His companion

116

seemed interested in everything he said. Lily was learning, and Buck was sharing, both of them absorbed.

Buck interrupted himself to hold up his mug. The waitress, a muscular woman with slightly orange hair, pushed away from the counter and picked up the glass coffee pot. She ambled over and refilled Buck's mug, then Lily's. She looked ready to drop.

"Another beer, too, huh?" Buck said softly.

"Make that *dos*." Lily held up two fingers, in case the waitress didn't understand Spanish.

"I ain't that dumb, honey."

Buck and Lily exchanged grins, amused by the woman's surliness. Dawn wasn't the best time of day for everybody, as it was for Buck. For Lily, too, judging from the way she threw back her beer, sausage, and eggs and kept going. She had stamina to match his, and that was more than Buck could say for the other band members.

"Yeah," he said, "we played in some pretty funky places, Garland and me. Some of 'em used to have chicken-wire fence up between the customers and the band, to catch the beer bottles and stuff they'd git to throwing at us. If you played a song reminding some fella of his ex-ol' lady, or somethin' else he didn't like, you could get your head handed to you."

Lily laughed out loud. Buck took his beer from the waitress and nodded.

"No joke," he added, remembering. "Sometimes it was downright terrifyin'."

Lily's laughter trailed off. They sat waiting for the waitress to take away the plates, but after that they still didn't speak. The drunk had dropped a quarter into the juke box, and the sound of Buck's voice singing "Good-Hearted Woman" filled the diner. Buck was touched by the coincidence but

117

glad that no one recognized him. Sometimes it was nice to be nobody special, sitting in an all-night diner in Oklahoma City, waiting for the sun.

When the song was over, Lily said, "They want you to quit, don't they?"

Buck nodded. He didn't want to discuss that topic.

"And you're thinkin' about it?"

He shrugged. A girl in her twenties couldn't understand the complications involved.

"I know mama made Garland quit," she said. "And I understand her side of it. But Garland isn't you, Buck."

"No offense, Lily, but this is somethin' between my family and me." Loyalty wasn't all. Buck didn't like to be lectured. "You're just a kid. You don't know about—obligations." Now he was doing the lecturing.

"If I was just a kid, you wouldn't look at me like you did back there in that motel room."

Buck felt his resistance going. The only way to get her to back off and spare them both a lot of heartbreak was to insult her.

"At four o'clock in the morning," he said, "anything looks good sittin' on a motel room bed."

He saw right away that the insult had taken, because Lily flushed with anger. Her eyes narrowed, and Buck recognized some of Garland's temper there.

"I've been goin' to bed with a song of yours every night since I was twelve years old," she told him. "Mama always thought it was Garland I was listening to." She took a swallow of beer and brought the bottle down on the table hard enough to attract attention. "I've always been scared to death you'd get old before I grew up. Shit!" The waitress and the cook were watching them, and now the drunk's head came up off the counter.

"And the last coupl'a days," Lily went on, "I've been so happy 'cause I figured I'd made it in just under the wire."

By being loyal to Viv and Jamie, Buck was shortchanging Lily. Hers was no common infatuation.

"I've been livin' with you almost as long as Viv has," she said. "You just never knew it."

Buck looked down at his left hand, unable to meet her gaze. He examined the calluses on each of his fretting fingers. He felt like everyone in the diner was waiting for his reply.

"Anyway," Lily went on, "what's so real about biology and chronology? My soul might be twice as old as you are!"

The idea made him laugh. "You learn those big words in college?"

"Oh." She began to poke gentle fun at Buck. She turned to her little audience and smiled. "Suddenly he's just a simple country boy," she said, "with a knack for picking out notes on a guitar, folks." Then she put on a thick, Southern, cornpone accent. "Land sakes alive, Buck Bonham. You are a caution."

Buck liked her changes, her intensity, and her sense of humor. That wasn't all he liked, either. "Oh, boy," he sighed. Lily seemed older than he, and more in control.

She gave him a big wink and made a clicking sound with her tongue, vamping him in front of the others, pretending to be a sexy little groupie. Buck found that he no longer minded. In fact, that was just the trouble.

He swept his long hair back with both hands, then reached for the check.

They walked back to the motel, into the rising sun. Lily slipped her arm through Buck's and looked behind them. The lighted neon of the diner's sign stood out against the dark buildings; up ahead, the pinkish light reflected in the windows of the city. The scene reminded her of the cover of Bob Dylan's "Freewheelin'" album, except that it—the street, the sunlight, the exhilaration—belonged to her and to Buck. The words of the song "Yesterday's Wine" kept running through her mind.

Buck came into her room with her, as she knew he would. She took the joint out of the telephone book, where she had hidden it, and the two of them sat cross-legged in the middle of the bed and smoked it. They passed the joint back and forth until it was gone, and the drug had filled her with a warm, tingling sensation.

Buck said, "Sure does get rid'a the world, doesn't it?"

She nodded and took his hand in hers. She had been looking forward to this moment for years, and she was not going to let him out of her grasp.

They stared into each other's eyes for a very long time.

"It must be strange," Lily whispered, "being everybody's hero."

"It has its rewards."

"Take me—I'm one of 'em."

He moved toward her, and she met him halfway. They kissed lightly but held the kiss for what seemed like minutes. Then without a word they got up and began to undress.

Buck beat her between the sheets. Men always were faster than women, for some reason. He lay there and watched her in the half-light as she stepped out of her Levis and slipped in next to him.

"God," he said, "I'm gonna roast in hell for this one."

Honeysuckle Rose

She felt no guilt at all, just fulfillment and a crazy kind of happiness.

"You tell anybody about this," he added, taking her in his arms, "and I'll have you shot."

"I'm having a T-shirt printed up: Buck Bonham Slept Here."

He kissed her lips, neck, shoulder, breasts. Lily urged him to mount her. She put her arms around his lean, hard body and raised her hips to meet him. She was swollen and damp from the anticipation, and the drug had left her sensitive to the barest touch.

She cried out when he entered her, but not from pain.

14

Buck turned from the audience and sought out Lily with his eyes. The slow tempo of the song fit his mood exactly, and for a few seconds he could believe that they were the only two people in the auditorium. The lights and the smoke and the undercurrent of voices that never ceased entirely during any concert faded before a rush of memories from that day at dawn.

At the end of the song, applause shattered the mood, but not the affection they both felt. Neither of them looked away. Buck knew that Bonnie would notice something different in the way he and Lily regarded one another, but he didn't care. He struck an idle chord on his guitar and broke into an entirely different mood and tempo, one that drove the audience into another round of applause.

Buck laughed as he sang, talking to Lily with his eyes, enjoying himself. He knew Lily shared his high in performing, the satisfaction he felt in playing well and hearing approval from the crowd. It was the only thing that mattered then.

He beckoned to Lily with his head. She balked, uncertain of what he wanted. He beckoned her forward again, and she reluctantly came, just as the music trailed off.

Buck turned to the microphone. "We have a new guitar player this time around." He made it sound casual and professional: Lily was a real member of the band. "Lily Ramsey!"

The fans clapped and whistled, and Lily bowed to their enthusiasm.

"Plays pretty good for a girl, huh?" said Buck, winking at her. "Lily comes from a musical family." He played a few idle chords and added, "Lily's Garland Ramsey's daughter."

This time the crowd roared its approval. They knew Garland, but they also recognized talent when they heard it, and Buck slipped easily into the next song, with Lily still at his side.

The bus sped north, through the night. Lily rode shotgun, next to Buck, listening to the banter among the band members. They were unwinding with beer and bologna sandwiches put together by Bo, who stood in front of the little galley, his feet wide-spread for balance.

"Did you see those two guys fighting down front tonight?"

"Did you see that girl dancing with her shirt off and her jeans unzipped?" Rooster wanted to know.

"As loaded as I was," Bo admitted, "I couldn't tell the difference."

"I could," Tex said. "The two that was fightin' had hair on their heads."

The boys all laughed.

Bonnie looked up from her needlepoint. "If it wasn't for bad taste, you guys'd have no taste at all."

Jonas asked Bo, "Remember where I do that break—*ch gung ch gung ch gung, dit dit dit*—only faster?"

Lily wondered what ordinary people would think, listening to musicians talk. She understood what Jonas was talking about, but few other people would. Musicians were a race all to themselves.

"You should come in there," Jonas said.

"Where?" asked Bo.

Jonas pretended he was playing his guitar, holding a sandwich in his left hand and a beer in his right. "When I go *dit dit dit.*"

"Oh." Bo nodded solemnly.

Lily had wanted to be accepted by the band, and she had been. But she would rather have been alone with Buck.

"Don't you love driving at night?" she asked.

Buck just smiled. She had a strong urge to touch him, a feeling that had come over her several times that night, and she had to restrain herself.

"Maybe," she added, "we could just saw the bus right off behind this seat and just keep on driving."

Buck looked at her reproachfully.

"I mean just for a month or two." She knew he would understand. "We could sleep in the fields and stay up all night drinking and singing for our supper in the little taverns and stuff."

"Yeah," Buck said wistfully, "that's the way it ought'a be."

Lily didn't want to make him sad. His moods were changeable, like his music. She picked up her guitar from the seat behind them and began to pick.

"Wanna hear a song I wrote?" It took courage for her to play it in front of the great Buck Bonham. "It isn't about you, but it could be."

Lily didn't wait for an answer. Softly she sang the words that had been forming in her mind since the tour began for her, words about wandering and a person's need to test himself. She looked straight ahead while she played, watching the highway markers rise up out of the darkness, aware of the laughter and the talking in the background. The distances of the plains beyond the windows of the bus held her attention and lent real meaning to her song.

She finished and looked over at Buck. She could tell that she had touched him.

"Maybe you better cool it on the romance," he said. "I wouldn't want anybody to get the right idea."

Lily put the guitar back on the seat. "Lemme drive," she said, feeling her own mood lighten. "I drove an eighteen-wheeler once, hitchhiking back from school. And I only took down one stop sign and a mailbox. . . ."

They crept into bed together shortly after daybreak, in a motel on the outskirts of Tulsa. They made love, and they slept, and then they made love again. They ate breakfast sitting up in bed together, pretending to be a middle-aged married couple from New Jersey. They laughed until they spilled coffee on the sheets. Buck had hung out the DO NOT DISTURB sign; he hoped the telephone would never ring.

Later they went walking in a shopping mall near the motel. The mood persisted. In a clothing store Buck tried on a bright yellow blazer designed for a golfer. He knew he looked ridiculous in the blazer, with his pigtails, his leathery skin, and his Levis, but he pretended that he was interested in buying it when a clerk came scurrying toward him.

"That looks nice," the clerk said.

Lily could barely stifle her laughter. Buck stepped in front of a mirror, turned one way and then the other, appraising himself. He took a pair of red-white-and-blue Madras slacks from a hanger and held them up. The clerk continued to nod.

Lily went into another department and came

back with a green Tyrolean hat with a feather stuck in the band. Buck put it on. In the mirror he saw the reflection of what might have been a Bavarian Indian chief.

"How do you like this, Lily?"

"You look like Arnold Palmer on acid or something."

Even the clerk was forced to smile.

"Lemme think about this," Buck said, dumping the clothes into his arms. "Maybe I'll be back later."

Hand in hand, they walked back to the motel.

15

Viv and the other people involved in planning the Labor Day concert met at the bowling alley. It was never crowded in the afternoons, and the tables were big enough for the lanky contractor to spread out his plans. The bowling alley also had the best hamburgers in Austin, except the Raw Deal Café.

Garland and Rosella came in while Viv was going over the sketches for the stage and the scaffolding that was to hold the lights and the speakers. Outdoor concerts of the size they had in mind took a lot of preparation, and she had been making notes for days. With the Ramseys was an accountant in a polyester shirt, the long-haired stage manager in a cowboy hat that the band had used before, and a young woman from a local advertising agency. She had brought mock-ups of the posters for the group's approval. She spread them out on the table, and they anchored the corners with beer cans.

"Now these are just the proofs," the young woman said. "The colors will be a little different in this one." She pointed to the biggest photograph of Buck, his unbraided hair held in a headband, his lips compressed in an attitude of concentration that Viv knew well. "And the other one needs larger lettering."

127

"That ain't a good picture of Buck," the contractor said. "He ain't that serious."

They all laughed, and Viv joined in. But she didn't share their gaiety. The excitement of the annual concert hadn't gotten to her yet, although she was sure it would once the plans got underway. For years—ever since she had stopped traveling with the band—Viv had instinctively assumed the role of coordinator for the Labor Day event, just as she instinctively handled the business when Sid was on the road. It was something that needed doing, and she did it, without expecting thanks or praise. Buck and the others were incapable of looking after their own affairs; that was just one reason why she loved them all.

Viv felt close to the band, even when they were five hundred miles away. Over the years she had developed a kind of sixth sense about the progress, following them in her mind from stand to stand, imagining them unpacking their equipment, then packing up again and driving on. Buck's telephone calls kept her in almost constant touch. But this time she hadn't heard from him in two weeks.

The stage manager was talking to her. "We're getting all the lights from Sho-Con, in Dallas. And the sound stuff, we have all of it here in Austin."

"Did you talk to those record people this afternoon?" she asked. "They called me." People in the music business were always calling Viv.

"I hate talkin' to anybody from Los Angeles about anything. I think we oughta keep this small."

"Small?" The accountant laughed and shook his head. "Walter over here just ordered thirty-six portable toilets."

The contractor affirmed it. The concert was going to be anything but small. "We'll have all the power in there by Thursday," he said. "By the way,

Viv, ol' Harvey Cline's expecting a check from you before he runs that main line in to us."

Viv made a note. She was beginning to feel overloaded with details.

"A check?" the accountant said. "Harvey seems to have forgotten all the money Buck loaned him two years ago when his wife was sick and he was about to go bankrupt. He still owes Buck about fifteen hundred dollars."

"I always told Buck that if he didn't stay out there makin' money to loan out or give away, half this county'd have to go on welfare."

Viv was well aware of her husband's generosity. His good fortune was everybody's good fortune, although sometimes he gave away money that the family could well have used. Buck would laugh at Viv if she complained. It helps to stay a little hungry, he always said.

Garland held up one of the posters. "They're nice," he said, but there was doubt in his voice. He eyed the big letters that spelled out *Concert in Honor of Garland Ramsey.* "Sounds like I'm dead."

They all got a kick out of that. Viv wondered if Garland missed traveling. He seemed happy enough, but she could not imagine Buck making that transition without some hard times to go with it.

A young man with long, curly blond hair approached the group. He smiled awkwardly, waiting for Rosella to notice him.

Finally he said, " 'Scuse me, Mrs. Ramsey, but have you heard from Lily? How's she doing out there?"

"She called after her first concert, Dorsey. But we haven't heard from her since."

"Well, if you hear from her," the young man said, "tell her we miss her."

He walked off, looking lost. Viv assumed he

129

was Lily's boyfriend, and she felt a little sorry for him. Then she realized that she should also be feeling sorry for herself.

Rosella asked Viv, "Have you heard from Buck?"

"No, I expect he'll call tonight. Or maybe tomorrow."

The band was just on a tight schedule, she thought.

When the telephone rang at the ranch the next day, Viv was certain it was Buck calling. So was Jamie. He lay on the living room rug, thumbing through a magazine about horses, and he looked up expectantly. Viv grabbed the phone and said, "Hello, Bonhams."

To her disappointment, a strange voice asked if hers was the number for Buck Bonham's Band.

"Yes," she said, with a lot less enthusiasm.

"Is it papa?" Jamie asked.

Viv shook her head. It was Cotton Roberts's manager, calling to say that his boy would be available sooner than they had thought.

"When's he going to be free now? After Baton Rouge?"

Sooner, the man said. After Reno.

"Oh," Viv said, trying to remember Buck's schedule. "Well, that's a couple days early, but he could catch up with Buck in—"

She left him on the line and picked up a printed itinerary from the pile of posters, sketches, and date books in the middle of the table. Jamie had already lost interest in the conversation, realizing that it was just "business." Viv felt a touch of resentment at having to talk to this man, instead of to her husband.

"St. Louis, I guess," she told the manager. "Or the sixteenth and seventeenth in—"

As she ran a finger down the schedule, she had one happy thought. Now she would have an excuse to call Buck, if Sid didn't call her first.

Buck leaned on his pool cue and watched Lily line up her shot. The tattered lamp shade hung low over the pool table, the lightbulb casting stark shadows on the worn green felt. An old Hank Williams record was playing on the jukebox, and a Lone Star sign winked on and off behind the bar, like a beacon. Buck had stopped in the café many times to drink beer, eat homemade chili, and shoot some eight-ball, while the bus was being gassed up outside and the band members given time to stretch. They were eating and having a good time in the worn wooden booths that ran the length of the narrow room, just like old times. Buck could remember standing in that same spot twenty years before, just like yesterday. The big difference now was Lily.

She made her shot, following through like a professional. The faded thirteen ball rolled lazily across the table and dropped into the corner pocket.

Buck was delighted. "Get another one. Let 'em know what they're up against."

Lily didn't even smile. She and Buck were playing Tex and Kelly, and Lily was determined to win. She lined up another shot, standing on one foot and stretching so that she was almost prone on the table, squinting along the length of her cue. But this time the ball touched the railing and hung in the mouth of the pocket without falling in.

She looked up at Buck. "Sorry."

"That's all right," Buck said quickly. "Damn table's leaning. Your shot, Kelly."

Kelly lined up a combination involving the eight-ball, a risky proposition. While he studied it,

131

Tex winked at the waitress behind the counter, and Buck saw the waitress wink back. Tex took a drag on his Bobby Burns, the cigar's tip glowing red, and blew a large, perfect smoke ring. Then he pushed his finger inside the ring, raising his eyebrows. Buck thought the waitress was going to swoon.

Sid walked up to the table. He had been outside in the phone booth. "Buck—"

"Yeah," Buck said, cutting him off. "Just a minute." Buck wanted to see the shot.

Kelly plowed into the cluster of balls. The three-ball bounced off the eight-ball and wobbled into the side pocket. Cheers went up from the booths.

"Well," Buck said appreciatively, "kiss a duck's bright red hiney." It was an expression of great respect.

Sid sidled up to Buck. "I just talked to Viv," he whispered. "Cotton Roberts was canceled out in Reno. He's gonna meet us in St. Louis Thursday."

Buck had forgotten all about Cotton Roberts. "Hey, Lily's doin' good. What do we need him for?"

Sid rolled his eyes. He always did that when he thought Buck was being unreasonable.

But Buck was thinking about Lily and the sudden sense of loss that had come over him.

In the meantime, Kelly had missed his shot, leaving the way open to victory.

"All right, Buck," Lily called out happily, "run the table on 'em."

"Shoot for me, will you, Lily?"

Buck and Sid stepped over to the counter. Sid turned his back to the others.

"Viv made a deal with the guy," he said, "and he quit his other band 'n all. We'll probably get sued if you cancel him now."

That was true. Buck didn't mind going to court, but there were Viv and the band to think about.

"You want me to tell Lily?" Sid asked.

"No, I better do it."

He went back to the table. Lily was about to shoot, but she paused before the stroke and looked up at him. They stared at each other. Then she said simply, "Cotton Roberts?"

Buck would have preferred to tell her when they were alone, but it was too late. He nodded.

Lily went back to her shot as if nothing had happened. But Buck saw the tears gather in her eyes, and so did the others.

Suddenly they all lost interest in pool.

The lights dimmed, and the faces in the audience receded into the darkness. Lily could hardly believe that just two weeks before she had been terrified of all the people; now she was terrified of losing them. Her life in that short time had become a perfect blend of artistic expression, recognition, and love. The alternative to it, glimpsed that afternoon in Buck's eyes, filled her with an enormous sadness.

It was her last concert. Instinctively, she began to sing softly along with Buck.

> I have never gone so wrong
> As telling lies to you.
> What you see is what I've been.

Buck turned from the mike and smiled at her. Embarrassed, Lily stopped singing.

"No," he said, "it's all right. Come on up here."

She hesitated. It was an honor to sing with Buck at the mike, and a serious responsibility, but she wanted to be close to him. If Buck liked her, then the audience would, too.

He beckoned again, and she joined him.

Lily felt that the words spoke just to her. When she sang, it was Buck's voice she heard, Buck's eyes she saw.

They were making love to the music, with their voices and their eyes. Lily felt warm and private, even though a thousand people watched them. The audience, the band members, Sid and the others standing in the wings couldn't help but notice what was taking place between Buck and her. But she didn't care. A veil of light and sound surrounded and protected them, lifting them up and carrying them to some distant, still place. Lily knew they were untouchable that night, and only that night.

16

Sid ordered a Bloody Mary and leaned back against the red plush banquette in the motel lounge. Sunlight cut through the gloom, and the sound of Muzak blocked out the conversation of other people having drinks. Sid looked around the room, trying to spot Cotton Roberts's manager. Sid and Buck had agreed to meet him there, to take care of business before the guitar player made his appearance.

Buck slumped in a chair across the table, looking as out of place as a renegade Indian at a charity ball. They were no longer in the West, and Buck's Levis, headband, and long braided hair were curiosities in St. Louis. Many of the people at the tables around them recognized Buck, and those who didn't seemed to think they should. Buck, as always, was oblivious of the attention he attracted. He looked tired and depressed. Sid could easily imagine why.

Sid picked up the glass the waitress brought him and took a long drink. He was feeling better but was careful not to show it. The fact that Cotton Roberts was joining the band early was a real stroke of luck. Sid liked Lily, and he liked the way she played; she had enough talent to become a permanent member, but talent wasn't the problem. Infatuation was. It didn't take a genius to see that she and Buck had fallen for each other in a big way. Girls were supposed to fall for country stars, but Buck's behavior surprised him. Sid had traveled with him long enough to know that Buck wasn't casual with his relationships. This time Viv stood on one side and Garland on the other, and there was potential trouble everywhere. It might not just break up Buck's marriage, it might also break up the band.

Sid saw the manager then. He approached their table, taking short, quick strides, the heavy gold chain around his neck bouncing against a soft, hairy expanse of chest. In addition to the open shirt, he wore aviator glasses with tinted lenses that completed his California look. His hair was long and slightly oily, and his loafers had little gold stirrups across the insteps.

They exchanged greetings. The manager grabbed Sid's hand and began to pump it, at the same time patting Buck on the back.

"Hell," he said, "you don't know how much Cotton and I admire your music, Buck. Just all to hell nuts about it, no lie." He pulled out a chair and dropped into it. "You are an original, I guarantee it."

Sid and Buck exchanged glances. Sid looked down at the floor. He moved his feet as if he had stepped in the middle of a large, fresh cow patty, and held up one boot to inspect it for damage. But Buck accepted the praise with a smile.

"How 'bout a drink?" Buck said. "Where's yer boy hidin'?"

"He'll be right down. He wanted to clean up before he shook hands with his idol."

The waitress appeared. The manager told her curtly, "Double scotch, honey." She turned away, and he added, "Nice tits!"

The remark wasn't lost on the waitress, who

curled her lip in disgust. Buck and Sid regarded the manager evenly. They had come up against his type before—the hustler who would try to suck extra money out of the band for his client. Sid was there to make sure he didn't succeed.

"Now I did strike a deal with your wife," the man said, "for pay 'n all. But we never did get a chance to talk fringe."

"What's fringe?" asked Sid.

"Well, I'm talking about percent."

Buck leaned back and folded his arms across his chest, leaving the field to Sid. He would watch the hustle as if it were a tap-dancing act; Buck could always find something to amuse him.

"Percent of what?" said Sid.

"Gate, records, whatever you got. I got a new merchandising outfit—for T-shirts, posters . . ."

Sid and Buck remained silent. They knew the act wasn't over yet; there was no point in saying no until the curtain came down.

"I come up with a flash last night," the manager said. He leaned over the table, looking conspiratorial. "Why don't we buy us a load of Texas hats from Hong Kong or someplace? Straw wouldn't be but about eighty-five cents apiece from those Chinks. Put a crest on it"—he smiled as if the idea had just come to him—"a picture of Buck and Cotton! Sell 'em at the concerts."

Sid wasn't listening. His eyes had been drawn to the door by the sight of a big beaver-skin hat and a red-white-and-blue cowboy suit covered with sequins. Sid's heart sank. Cotton Roberts was wearing the kind of star-spangled Nashville high-hype outfit that Buck and the other band members had avoided all their professional lives.

Roberts walked up to the table and swept off his hat. He had a baby face and prematurely white hair in curled locks that tumbled to his shoulders.

Buck and Sid exchanged glances. Sid already knew what the outcome of the meeting would be. Cotton Roberts would play backup guitar for the rest of the summer tour, and then they would have to hire themselves a permanent picker. Next time Sid would give that choice a little more thought.

He and Buck stood up to shake hands. The manager made the introductions; it was clear that he did most of Cotton's talking for him. Cotton just grinned and snapped his chewing gum.

"That's quite a suit," Buck said.

Cotton nodded, running an appreciative hand over the satiny material.

"We bought half a dozen of 'em," said his manager. "Straight from Nudie's in Los Angeles." He strung out the *e* at the end of the word making it sound like "Angelees". "Cost us a fortune, I guarantee it."

Cotton caught the waitress by the arm and whispered a command in her ear. Finally he sat down. "Real great," he said, propping his red boots on a chair.

"You wear them outfits on stage?" Buck asked.

"Hell, yeah," the manager said. "Lights hit them shiny things, it damn near blinds 'em for ten rows back."

Buck chewed on his lower lip, keeping his own counsel about Cotton's wardrobe.

Sid didn't know what the hell to say.

They all rode up together in the elevator. Buck was determined to get rid of Cotton one way or another. A plan was already forming in his mind, one that appealed to his sense of humor. He knew better than to reveal it to Sid.

"Catch you later, stud," Cotton said as they stepped out onto the top floor.

"You bet," Buck told him.

"We'll be moving the bus out of here 'bout seven-thirty," said Sid. "On stage at eight-thirty, okay?"

"Nice doin' business with ya." The manager clapped Sid on the shoulder. "You're good people, hey!"

He and Cotton sauntered off.

"I made a plane reservation for Lily for tomorrow morning," Sid said. "I'm gonna go tell her."

Buck walked along with him. There was no need for conversation between them about Cotton Roberts and his manager.

"Let her play tonight, huh?" Buck said. "In case this fella Roberts can't cut it or somethin' goes wrong." Sid started to object, but Buck interrupted him. "Say, how much money you got on ya?"

"A bunch."

Buck knocked on the door. "Lily, open up!" Then he told Sid casually, "Gimme about five hundred bucks."

Sid looked skeptical. But he dug down into his pocket for the roll of cash.

Lily opened the door. "Hi," she said, and she smiled, but Buck knew that she was torn up inside. "I understand my replacement arrived."

"Yeah," said Buck. "Listen, let's you and me go for a walk."

Sid handed him a wad of bills. "What the hell you need five hundred bucks for?"

Buck gave him a look that shut him up. Then he took Lily's arm and started back toward the elevator.

Sid drove the band members to the concert hall an hour before the curtain. Cotton Roberts and his manager sat together in the front of the bus and weren't too sociable; Cotton was playing the role of star. His sequined cowboy outfit elicited smiles among the other musicians, but no one said anything.

Sid went into the office to talk to the promoter and to check on the receipts. When he returned backstage, there was no sign of Buck or the rest of the band. Tex's drums had been set up, and guitars and basses lay about on the boards among the mike wires, but there were no people.

He couldn't understand it. The hall was filled to the seams, and the fans began to clap good-naturedly and stomp their feet. It was the sort of situation that gave managers ulcers.

Cotton and his manager stood in the wings. Cotton held a molded electric guitar with sparkles built into the plastic.

"Where's Buck?" Sid asked. "Anybody seen the band? We're ten minutes late already."

They both shrugged; it wasn't their problem. Cotton made final adjustments on his silver guitar strap.

Sid checked his watch again. The clapping had grown louder. When he looked up, he saw Buck crossing the stage, as casual as he could be.

"Where were you?" Sid asked. "We gotta go on."

Buck ignored the question. "Say, Cotton," he said, "go on out there and warm 'em up a little, will ya? Just do whatever you want. Do some of yer own stuff, huh?"

"What?" said Sid. He couldn't believe it; Buck never used a warm-up.

"Leave the curtain shut," Buck went on. "Just go out 'n play 'em a coupl'a songs. You can handle that, can't ya?"

"Are you kidding?" The manager was insulted.

"Handle it? He'll have 'em in the aisles on the second song."

"First song," Cotton corrected. He snapped his gum.

Buck told Sid to take the manager out into the hall so they could see Cotton perform along with the audience. Sid knew something was wrong then, but he didn't object. The two of them went out and sat in the house seats. Sid's stomach was full of butterflies; he wondered what Buck was up to.

Cotton stepped out onto the apron of the stage, and the crowd applauded. They were ready to hear music, even if it was played by a dude in a star-spangled rodeo outfit. He had a vocal mike and another for his acoustic guitar. He sang a little song, the sequins flashing in the spotlight.

"Well, thank ya, cousins," Cotton said, when the applause had died down. "Now, gee, ain't that sweeter'n Dolly Parton in a bucket of buttermilk."

The audience laughed, but they were not standing in the aisles, as Cotton had predicted. He decided not to sing another song.

"Now here's the man I came here to play with," he announced. "Buck Bonham!"

After a delay the curtain jerked open. The band broke into the familiar opening of "Whiskey River," but for several seconds the audience sat in stunned silence. Then the concert hall filled with whoops and catcalls, for Buck and Lily, Bonnie, and the rest of the band members were dressed like golfers. They wore mismatched Madras slacks, and blazers of bright, garish colors. Their cowboy hats had been replaced by outlandish styles in straw or felt with little brims. Buck wore a pointed green Tyrolean pulled down around his ears, his pigtails mashed flat against his head, and black-and-white wing-tip shoes.

Cotton Roberts stood and stared, mouth open, eyes wide. Then he stomped off the stage, dragging the guitar wire behind him.

Sid understood why Buck had needed the five hundred dollars. The manager was pushing at him, trying to get back out into the aisle. Sid wanted to explain that it was just a joke, but he couldn't stop laughing.

Buck and the rest of the band gathered in the dressing room after the concert and dumped their new clothes into a big cardboard box. He doubted if he could get a refund on the outfits, but he didn't really care. The fun had been worth the expense, and he was rid of Cotton Roberts.

Rooster handed around beer, and Buck passed a joint. He was unlacing his wing-tip shoes when the door flew open. Cotton and his manager walked in without invitation, followed by two beefy "roadies"—men hired by Cotton to carry his equipment and protect him from his fans. Cotton was mad, but Buck had expected that.

"You son of a bitch!" Cotton shouted, his white locks dancing. "You made me look like a fool out there."

Buck went back to his shoelaces. "I didn't make you wear that suit."

"I oughta bust you in the nose."

Cotton stood over him, his fists clenched, the roadies at his elbows. Buck stood up slowly and looked him in the eye.

"Hey," Lily said, stepping between them, "it was just a little gag."

"Shut up, bitch." Cotton looked her up and down, and Buck felt his blood begin to boil. "It's easy to see how you got your job, and it obviously wasn't with a guitar, unless you play it in bed."

Buck didn't hesitate. He hit Cotton with a

142

right cross that caught him flat on his button nose.
Cotton fairly leaped backwards over a chair, more
afraid of disfigurement than insult, and his manager and the roadies rushed forward. Tex hit one of
the roadies with a malletlike left hook. He went
down, scattering the folding chairs, while Bo and
the other roadie traded punches like professionals,
waltzing up and down the dressing room. Sid and
Rooster grabbed the manager and hurled him toward the door. The first roadie got up and hit Tex
in the stomach with his head. They tumbled onto
the box of new clothes, flattening it. They rolled
around on the floor. Kelly, still drinking his beer,
jumped to avoid their thrashing feet.

Security guards drawn by the noise came into
the room and began to break up the fights. Buck
waited for Cotton to come back at him, but he
seemed to have lost his appetite. He just stood
behind his bodyguards and sneered.

Lily touched Buck's arm. She looked fright-
ened and confused.

Buck took her by the shoulders and kissed her
full on the lips. He had decided it was time for
people to see how he felt about her.

Everybody, including Lily, was astounded.

"On top'a that," Buck said, grinning defiantly
at Cotton, "she plays better'n you do, *stud.*"

Cotton marched out of the room, followed by
the roadies. The manager turned and shook his fist
at Buck.

"I'll get you for this, you bastard!"

17

The clatter of hammers carried across the open pasture. The stage was almost complete, the new wood bright in the sunlight, surrounded by scaffolding on which the lights would be mounted. Viv was proud of those light towers. She had insisted on the extra height, and Steve, the stage manager, now agreed that they were an improvement over the previous year's. It got dark out there in the country on Labor Day night, and Viv wanted to make sure people could see where they were going, as well as the antics of Buck and the band.

Everywhere she looked, there was activity. The electricians were stringing cable, and a man on a Caterpillar tractor towed a string of fiberglass privies through the field, dropping them off at strategic locations. It looked like the site would be ready on schedule.

Viv had done all the contracting herself, to cut expenses. In one hand she held a stack of pay envelopes, in the other, a cigarette. She left the pickup parked at the top of the hill and walked down toward the stage. Howard, the construction foreman, fell into step beside her, and Steve came running to join the inspection tour, his long hair flying beneath his hard hat.

144

"Well," Steve said, "not much more to do now, Viv. The lights start coming in tomorrow."

Viv nodded. She already knew about the lights.

"You've done a great job," Howard told her. "Any time you want to go into the construction business, Viv, you can run my office."

The carpenters interrupted their work to wave to her. Viv knew most of them by name.

"You get your permit problems straightened out?" Steve asked.

"Yeah," she said. The liquor license had been a real pain. "Not much to do now but order the food and the beer." She waved to a workman up on the tower. "Hi, Jim."

He called down to her. "Say, Viv, me and the boys got you somethin' for all your hard work."

He reached down and picked up something from the platform.

"Catch!"

He tossed a piece of cloth into the air. It fluttered toward the ground like a heavy leaf, and Viv caught it. She spread the cloth out and saw that it was a T-shirt. Printed on it in big red letters was the word Wonderwoman.

Viv was touched. "Aw, wonderful," she said. She waved to Jim and the others who were climbing down from the scaffolding. "Great!"

One of the men said, "Put it on."

That posed a problem. She wore a jumper, and she was not going to unbutton it in front of all the men. The T-shirt looked big to her, so she slipped it over her head and down over the dress.

She turned around, modeling it, and they all clapped.

"When's Buck and the band comin' back?"

"They have a couple more dates to do," she

145

said. It seemed like Buck had been gone for months. "I think I'm goin' to go surprise him in Phoenix tomorrow night and then come back with him. If you all can get along without me."

Buck had told her to surprise him; everybody thought it was a good idea.

"Go bring them boys home," Jim said. "We'll be ready for 'em."

> Turning on the world the way she smiles
> Upon my soul as I lay dying;
> Healing as the colors in the sunshine
> And the shadows of her eyes.

The music drifted into the kitchen from Jamie's room, where he had the radio tuned to Buck's live broadcast in Santa Fe. Putting away the last of the supper dishes, she hummed along, aware that something was not right. Then she realized what it was: Buck was not singing alone. He was singing a duet with a woman, and that woman was Lily.

Viv went over the band's travel itinerary in her mind. After St. Louis they had played Kansas City and now Santa Fe. Cotton Roberts should already have joined up with the band, and Lily should have been back in Austin.

She went and peered into Jamie's room, to see if he was asleep. But he lay on his back on the bed, playing with his BB gun, wearing pajamas and his habitual boots. She flicked the light switch up and down.

"Closing time, buckeroo. Lights out."

"Lily's singing with papa," Jamie said. He was pleased about it.

"She's moving up in the world." Viv thought the duet sounded sweet and heartfelt.

> Loving her was easier than anything
> I'll ever do again;

Coming close together with a feeling
That I've never known before.

Finally the music faded, and a commercial for
Bull Durham chewing tobacco came on the air. Viv
turned off the radio and leaned down to kiss Jamie
on the nose.

"Go to sleep," she said.

She left his room and stood for a moment in
the dark hallway. The feeling of uneasiness would
not go away. She told herself that she was worried
about the possibility of Cotton Roberts missing his
connection with the band, but she knew it had
more to do with the sound of Buck's distant voice.

The telephone was ringing. At first she
thought it might be Buck but realized that was
impossible. Maybe it was Sid, calling to explain the
mix-up.

She ran into the living room and picked up the
receiver. "Hello."

The voice that answered was vaguely familiar
and slurred from too much whiskey. She hated to
receive calls from friends at night urging her to
come out and party. They made her feel lonelier
than ever.

"Viv, this is Cotton Roberts's manager. I just
want you to know you're married to a son of a
bitch, and Cotton is gonna sue him for breach of
contract, damages to his career . . ."

She started to hang up. Buck must have decided that Cotton wasn't up to his reputation and let
him go. Viv was interested in hearing the details,
but she wasn't going to listen to some drunk abuse
her husband. Then the manager said something
that changed her mind.

". . . and if you know what's good for you,
you'll look into what's goin' on between him and
that female guitar player he's got."

"What are you talkin' about?" she asked.

He hung up.

The dial tone sounded very loud to her. Gently she replaced the receiver, then turned on her radio. She tuned in the Santa Fe station. Buck and Lily were singing another duet, their voices pure and plaintive in the still evening air. The music was painful for her, but she forced herself to listen. She had put up with the long separations from Buck because she loved him, and she understood his needs. He was wild and unpredictable and exciting, and she could excuse most anything he did. But there were limits to any freedom, even that of a wandering guitar picker like her husband, and she drew the line at Lily Ramsey.

Viv was careful to give Buck the benefit of the doubt. She would wait until she could see for herself. Cotton Roberts's manager might well be lying.

But something told her he wasn't.

The flight from Austin to Phoenix took almost two hours. She left after dark. Dinner was served on the airplane, but the processed mashed potatoes and the anemic-looking filet mignon didn't tempt her. She had a martini, instead. Then she had another one. By the time she stepped down onto the Arizona tarmac, she was a little high.

She took a cab straight to the auditorium. The parking lot was jammed, and the auditorium doors were closed. Buck and the band were popular everywhere, it seemed—in the West, the South, the Midwest. Sid had talked of superstar status: Buck's time had come.

Viv could faintly hear him singing. It didn't sound like any song she knew.

The promoter in the front office—a short, fat man in white patent leather shoes—recognized her and led her down the empty corridor to the stage door. She could hear the words plainly now.

> If you're feelin' salty, I'm your tequila.
> If you've got the freedom, I've got the time.

Buck and Lily were singing an improvised lover's duet.

Viv stepped up into the darkened wings. Sid and Rooster stood directly in front of her, unaware of her presence. The crowd was reacting enthusiastically to the embarrassing lyrics. But Viv was not as interested in them as she was in the performers themselves. Buck and Lily stood facing one another at the mike, seemingly oblivious to their surroundings. Lily's hair had been braided into pigtails like Buck's, and she matched him word for word, chord for chord.

Viv felt an incalculable sadness. She considered turning around and leaving before she was noticed, flying back to Austin and pretending ignorance. But then the sadness began to give way to anger. Soon she was as mad as she had ever been.

> There ain't nothin' sweeter than naked emotions,
> So you show me yours, hon', 'n I'll show you
>   mine.

"Who picked that song," she asked, "him or her?"

Sid and Rooster spun around.

"Viv!" Sid sputtered. "What are you—doin' here?"

Both men stood rigidly at attention. Rooster looked like he was about to cry.

"Very tasteful lyrics," Viv said with heavy sarcasm. "Don't you think?"

"Ah—how was your flight?"

"Bumpy."

She stepped past them. Lily and Buck continued to sing, unaware of her presence, grinning at one another, their noses almost touching.

Darlin', if you think about a change of direction,
Lord, you'd be somethin' I'm lucky to find.
So show me yours, hon', and I'll show you mine.

The song trailed off, and the audience thundered its approval. Buck and Lily bowed together, holding hands. Without hesitating, Viv walked straight out onto the stage. The other band members saw her coming, but Buck and Lily did not, so engrossed were they in the crowd and in one another. Viv felt her heart pounding. She was vaguely aware of surprise and a kind of horror on the faces of Bonnie, Bo, Bliss, Jonas, Kelly, and Tex as she passed them. Viv was careful to smile and nod, as if nothing was the matter. She wasn't going to scream and rage; she had a better idea.

She stepped up behind Buck and Lily and gave her husband a kiss on the cheek.

Buck turned around, and his eyes grew large. He did a doubletake. She got some satisfaction out of his confusion.

"Viv!"

"Hello, Mr. Wonderful," she said sweetly. "Nice duet."

Lily stood there open-mouthed. Viv gave her a little wave and smiled, as if nothing was wrong and it was perfectly natural for her to walk out onto the stage in the middle of a performance.

Buck recovered enough to approach the microphone and say, as an introduction to the crowd, "Viv—my—ah, wife."

The audience applauded her. Viv nodded in

acknowledgment, thinking that the people out there would clap for anything.

"I'm sorry to just barge in like this," she said, into the mike, "but I was backstage, and—" She paused, smiling, and looked from Buck to Lily and back again. "Wasn't that a wonderful duet?"

Again the crowd signaled its approval, missing the sarcasm in Viv's voice. She was sure that Buck didn't miss it, however. He knew Viv wasn't part of the act, even if his fans didn't.

Viv put a hand on Buck's shoulder and another on Lily's.

"You know, Lily here is"—Viv almost lost her control then, and let the tears flow, but she went on calmly—"such a surprise. She's the daughter of Buck's and my best friend, Garland Ramsey."

This time the applause was louder.

"Lily even gives music lessons to our ten-year-old son, Jamie. We've known Lily since she was just a little girl in pigtails." Viv pretended to be surprised. "Oh, I see she's in pigtails tonight."

Lily's hand came up automatically and touched her hair. She looked terrified.

"How cute!" Viv said. "Well, I don't want to hold up the show. I just wanted to surprise my husband a little bit. See, we've been together fifteen years, and tonight I'd like to announce"—she paused for effect—"our divorce!"

A stunned silence filled the hall. Still smiling, Viv leaned to the mike one more time.

"Now isn't that the kind of thing that country songs are all about?"

She waved goodbye. She turned and walked past the band, past Sid and Rooster in the wings, down the stairs, and out into the long, empty corridor.

18

Buck stood in the middle of the stage, dazzled by the spotlights. He could hear the audience shifting uneasily, the sound of coughs and nervous talking as people reacted to Viv's announcement. Buck felt confused and sorrowful, but he was also full of admiration for Viv's performance. She was a pro.

He looked at Lily. Her face was devoid of expression. The warmth and the closeness that had existed between them minutes before was gone now, replaced by awkwardness and a kind of shame. She slipped the guitar strap over her head, carefully placed the instrument on the floor, and walked off the stage in the other direction. Buck knew she just wanted a place to hide.

He couldn't follow her. Buck was a pro; he had a responsibility to his fans and to the band that waited to follow his lead. But he couldn't think of anything to say.

Then a woman's voice carried from the back of the auditorium: "We still love you, Buck!"

People clapped and whistled, and he was grateful to her.

"Thanks," he said. "I think we better say good night right about here. Sorry about tonight, everybody. You shouldn't have been brought into this."

He couldn't go on singing. He glanced at Sid

in the wings, and the business manager hissed at one of the stagehands, "Pull the curtain, damn it!"

The curtain began to close. The audience was applauding again, trying to give Buck a good send-off, calling out to him in encouragement. He turned and walked past the band without looking at them.

Sid caught up to him at the edge of the stage. He blurted out, "I didn't know anything about it, Buck."

He didn't care. People were pouring onto the stage, the pretty girls and the hangers-on that Buck was acquainted with only by sight; their names seemed to change with every new city. They plucked at his clothing, as if nothing unusual had just taken place. He wanted to get out.

"Viv left, Buck." Rooster was panting. "I couldn't catch her. She got a cab."

That meant she was on her way back to the airport, back to Austin. Buck scanned the crowd, looking for a face. Fans milled about him in confusion, laughing and touching him. Buck pushed through, trailed by Sid and Rooster. A woman in a gold lamé suit caught him around the neck with an arm and kissed him on the cheek, but Buck ignored her.

"Where's Lily?" he asked.

No one knew.

The bus rattled through the darkness, on the outskirts of Phoenix, headed for the motel. Rooster drove slumped over the wheel, intent on the string of opposing headlights. For once he had not snapped a cassette onto the tape deck; no music drifted from the overhead speakers.

Buck rode up front, watching the darkened storefronts and the little cafés and cantinas whip past. Lily sat next to him, silent and preoccupied.

No one else spoke, either. The joshing and partying that usually followed a concert had been replaced by a vigil. They were all waiting for Buck to speak.

He kept his eyes on the street, thinking about the nightlife in the places they passed. Men would be drinking beer in long straight lines at the bar, with a few women mixed in. Smoke would hang in the air, and an old familiar song would be playing on the jukebox. There would be joking and a few arguments, but mostly people would be having a good time, content with their world. Buck wished he could join them. He wished he could be just anybody—not famous and not obligated—and walk into the Del Rio or the Red Lounge, order a Pearl or a Coors, and sit there until dawn.

He turned around to face the others and saw the bright coals of their cigarettes glowing in the semidarkness.

"I'm sorry about tonight," he said, loud enough for his voice to carry to the back of the bus. He looked down at Lily and added, "Everybody. This was wrong for all of this to happen."

It was going to be even harder than he thought. Buck was not good at apologizing.

"I guess some of us won't be real welcome back at—ah—Garland's picnic."

Tex and Kelly grunted; the thought had already occurred to them. Viv wouldn't keep the story to herself, figuring that Rosella and Garland had a right to know.

Buck looked over at his business manager. "Sid, you think we could just extend a little bit? Keep this tour going for a little longer?"

Sid just shrugged. Buck could tell that he and the others didn't like the idea, but he pushed on.

"Whyn't you get on the phone in the morning,"

he said, "and look into it. Might even be a time to see how we'd go over back East." Sid had always claimed they were ready to "go large." Now was the time to find out.

"If I was you," Tex said jokingly, "I'd think about the *Far* East."

A few of them laughed. It wasn't, Buck thought, what you would call a full-scale riot.

Lily curled up in the chair in her room and watched Buck pace the floor. He moved and talked with the confidence of a man accustomed to trouble, but she had been badly shaken by the night's events. It had all happened so fast. The embarrassment she had felt on stage wasn't equal to the sense of guilt that followed. She had caused pain to her father and mother, to Viv and Jamie, and, through them, to Buck himself. The thought that there was a connection between Buck and her and the rest of the world had never occurred to her. They had been traveling, loving, and performing in a vacuum, and Viv had shattered that illusion in a few moments.

"If you don't feel like touring right now," Buck was saying, "we could shoot down to Mexico. I know a quiet place that's good for hiding out."

He was full of suggestions, but Lily had no idea what she wanted to do. Her father would be angry enough to kill her—and Buck. All her friends and relatives would find out. Life was never going to be the same, for either of them.

She admitted, "I'm so embarrassed and guilty I can't think."

"You never figured something like this was bound to happen?"

She shook her head, fighting back the tears. "All I knew that was bound to happen was that you would look at me one night on stage and smile. And I would sing like an angel, and you would fall in love with me, and—everybody would scream and shout...." It sounded stupid now, talking about it. She waved an imaginary wand in the air, for what she had envisioned was a kind of fairy tale.

"Sounds impossible," she went on, determined to tell him, "but I wanted that so much. I never thought any further. Obviously, I didn't dare to. All I knew was you were being pressured to quit—as if nobody but me understood how important you are. I guess I thought I was Joan of Arc or somebody." She managed a smile. "And you were France."

The tears began to flow, in spite of everything she could do to stop them. They ran down her cheeks and dripped onto her shirt, and she bowed her head so Buck wouldn't see.

He knelt in front of her on the rug and took her hands in his. "Not France," he said softly, making fun of himself, "maybe Arkansas or Oklahoma."

He tilted her face upward. Lily tried to smile again, but this time she couldn't bring it off. She had been in love with Buck for as long as she could remember. For the first time, she began to wonder if that was a good thing.

"I was gonna tell her anyway that I couldn't quit the road. And that would have been the end of that." Buck got up and walked to the window. He stared out into the darkness, toward a billboard mounted on a building at the edge of the desert. "She just beat me to it."

Lily had never thought about Buck without Viv and Jamie. To her, that was just another life he had, totally separate from their time together. Now she knew the two were connected.

"So," he said, as if he had resolved something

156

once and for all in his own mind, "do you want to keep on touring—or go to Mexico?"

She couldn't answer him.

"Lily, when you fall for one person, you usually end up hurting somebody else."

It was the saddest thing he had ever said, even in his songs. And it was absolutely true.

They made love at dawn. Buck held her in his arms and entered her tenderly, almost speculatively, as if he were experiencing her for the first time. Lily ran her fingers over his back and through his hair, whispering his name. Buck finished quickly. He felt that she was receding from him, that some more vital part of her was already beyond his touch, and she was calling out to him from an ever-increasing distance.

Lily fell asleep, but Buck could not. He lay there in the morning light, in a strange room and in a strange city that in a way were as familiar to him as his own home. He was a traveler, and he was in love with a lady half his age. He could not look at or touch Lily and think of leaving her. She was his, and now everybody knew it. He remembered walking into the hotel in Kansas City, the day after St. Louis, and standing by the front desk with the rest of the band. Sid had been handing out room keys to each person. Buck had taken Lily's, tossing his own key back to the desk clerk, a clear indication that he and Lily were living together. That seemed like a long time ago.

He got out of bed and dressed, then left Lily sleeping in the room. He walked down the hall and knocked on Sid's door. He hoped Sid was already on the telephone, talking to promoters on the East Coast. Because of the difference in time, the offices would already be open there; maybe Sid could wrap something up before lunch.

No one came to the door.

Buck went down to the coffee shop. His business manager sat facing the window, reading a newspaper. Outside, the bus sat in the parking lot, the familiar Lone Star shining in the morning sunlight.

"Hey, Sid." Buck sat down across the table from him.

"Mornin', Buck." Sid didn't offer any information about the possibility of continuing the tour. He didn't look like he had slept well, either.

Buck waited for the waitress to pour him a cup of coffee. Then he asked, "You talk to any promoters yet?"

Sid shook his head. He stirred his coffee, reluctant to discuss the issue.

Buck said, "I was thinking we could line up some college dates, maybe."

"Are you okay, Buck?"

He was not prepared for that. Buck wanted to keep their discussion on the business at hand, without personal considerations. He was the leader of the band, and he wanted the tour extended. It was the only way out of their predicament, one he had brought about and would solve. They would go East to perform for a week or two and let things blow over in Austin. He didn't want to talk about how he felt.

"I feel bad for ya," said Sid.

"I feel bad for *you*." Buck grinned, trying to appear unconcerned. "But I warned you I'd manage to screw things up somehow."

"I can't sweep up after you on this one. I wish I could."

Embarrassed, Buck looked away. He was touched by Sid's admission and the magnitude of his own problems. Screwing up seemed to be a habit of Buck's, but he always survived.

Outside, the band members had gathered around the bus. Buck noticed that they were unloading their instruments and that their suitcases stood about on the pavement.

"Hey, what are those guys doing?"

"Unpacking the bus," Sid admitted. "We talked last night. They want to go back to play at Garland's picnic."

Buck stood up quickly, almost overturning his chair. "I'm not going back there."

He headed for the door, followed closely by Sid. The band would just have to put their gear back on the bus. They had always followed his lead before.

"They all tried to figure out how to stay neutral in this, Buck. But you got 'em in the middle."

Buck crossed the parking lot, walking fast. His friends all turned toward him, gripping the handles of their cases like a bunch of musicians come to audition, looking uneasy but determined. Buck scanned their faces, searching for some indication that they might change their minds. But he didn't find it.

Bo said, "Can't let Garland down, Buck."

"Any more'n he's been let down already," Bonnie added.

Buck chewed on his lip and nodded. There was nothing left for him to say.

"Buy 'em all plane tickets, Sid. Lily and I'll be takin' the bus. I'll give you a call next week."

He walked back into the motel alone.

Lily heard him put his key into the door. She stood in front of the mirror brushing her hair, and she closed her eyes for a moment, preparing herself for what was to come. Her packed suitcase lay on the bed, next to her guitar case, and her Levi jacket lay across them both.

The door opened, and Lily turned to him. Buck's eyes were red-rimmed. He looked exhausted but defiant. He didn't even notice her things on the bed, he was in such a hurry.

"The band's going back for Garland's picnic," he said, as if the news meant nothing to him. Lily already knew. Bonnie had called to tell her so that Lily could make up her mind. "I guess we're goin' to Mexico."

He sat down on the edge of the bed and picked up the telephone. "You want some breakfast sent up?" he asked.

Lily walked over and put a hand on his shoulder. With the other hand she gently took the receiver from him and replaced it in the cradle. Buck looked up at her, puzzled.

Now that he was in trouble, Lily was more powerfully attracted to him than ever. Buck really was an outlaw, she realized, even among his own kind. His sexuality was closely tied up with that fact, coming through in the sound of his voice when he sang and in the sight of him beneath the lights. But there were few people who would follow him wherever his wild, beautiful impulses led. Even Viv had not been one of them. Lily wasn't, either.

"I can't go to Mexico," she told him. "I'm gonna go back and face Viv and my parents."

It was the final straw. Buck physically drooped beneath the weight of her revelation. His mouth opened, but he said nothing, squinting up at her in disbelief. Lily imagined that she could see him aging, his tough, leathery skin taking on a pallor, the crows' feet at the edges of his eyes deepening, the steely gray streaks in his hair growing more pronounced. She had the distinct impression that she was destroying him, that they were destroying each other.

"Come with me," she said. "It's not right, running away."

"No, you come to Mexico with me."

"No!"

He hadn't even considered her request. She felt torn between his needs and what she knew to be right. Going home would eventually heal him, heal them both, and it hurt her that Buck dismissed her suggestion. He didn't *want* to be healed if that meant ending their relationship, their love. Making her choose between Mexico and home was the same as making her choose between him and the rest of the world. Lily had already made that decision.

Buck noticed her bag on the bed. He stared at the floor and ran his hands through his hair. "Jesus," he whispered, "I guess it's just not my day."

He stood up suddenly and walked past her, to the dresser. A tightly rolled joint lay among the loose change and the matches left over from some other city, and he picked it up and lit it. He closed his eyes and took a deep drag, sucking air in along with the smoke from the marijuana, to increase its impact. He seemed to take some solace from the drug.

"It's already hit the fan," he said, over his shoulder. "Why cut out on me now?"

Lily didn't feel that she was cutting out. She was doing what she had to do. "I thought about what you said last night, about when you love somebody, it's bound to hurt somebody else."

"I been tryin' to get around that one all my life."

"But—" She paused, wanting to say it right. She found it difficult arguing with Buck. He had so much more experience, and talent, than she did, but Lily had to go with her instincts. Even when it hurt them both.

"It it hurts this many people," she said, "it's got to be wrong."

He turned to her. "What about you and me?" It was the first time he had ever spoken to her in anger, and Lily winced. "Our hurtin' doesn't count?"

"Not as much as Viv and"—she knew she was going to cry, again—"Jamie. We caused all this."

The mention of Jamie's name softened his expression. He was silent, thinking about what she had said. Lily had found a hidden weakness in Buck's outlawry that she hoped would lead him home.

"Jamie's still my son," he said a little defensively, "much as he's ever been."

"Come back and face the music, Buck."

She was crying, but this time she ignored the tears. She pitied Buck, and she admired him for the risks he was willing to take.

"I will," he conceded, "when I'm up to it."

He took another lungful of the sweetish smoke and tossed the roach into the ashtray.

"Oh, Buck," she said, laughing in spite of the tears, "you look so wounded."

Lily went to him, put her arms around his waist, and pressed her face against his chest. Her tears made dark marks on the pale blue material of his work shirt. She felt the chill of the turquoise he wore around his neck on a silver chain, the roughness of his belt and worn Levis, the softness of his braided hair. He hesitated and then enveloped her in his arms.

"What was that line," she asked, "about the guy that was shot and stabbed and dying on the barroom floor? Play 'Honeysuckle Rose'?"

He laughed softly, a flash of his old, sad humor. "It was his fav'rit' song."

Lily understood what had been a mystery to her before. It was finished, but she still loved his music.

19

The Interstate highway leading south out of Phoenix passes across flat, rocky desert trapped between the Maricopa and the Superstition mountain ranges. The land sweeps up to tall, redrock mesas and falls away again to the parched, barren valley pointing down toward Mexico. By late summer, all vegetation has shriveled and died, and dust devils dance far out from the highway, plumes of rising sand against a hard blue sky. No trees relieve the harsh, jagged outlines of the mountains. The small towns blessed with water bloom, but the desert takes up again at their outskirts. Eagles wheel a thousand feet above the blinding surface of the road, which is flat and mostly straight and leads a driver to put his foot down and make time.

Buck passed the Casa Grande ruins doing seventy miles an hour. The old bus rattled but held the road. It seemed as big as a freight car to him, and just as windy, the seats squeaking because there was no one to sit in them, only Buck's bag and guitar case in the overhead baggage rack. There was no food in the refrigerator this trip, and no cases of beer, for Buck was the only one whose needs had to be met, and he was content with the six-pack of Coors at his side. That and a little marijuana, which sat smoldering in the ashtray. He had no one to talk to, but for once that didn't bother him. He tuned in a country music station out of Phoenix, the western-style picking coming in loud and clear until he had climbed through the Picacho Pass and the music began to fade out. Then he slipped a cassette of his own on the tape deck and turned the volume up as loud as Rooster ever had. He flipped the switch for the outdoor speakers, too, filling the wild, rugged countryside with the sound of Buck Bonham's Band.

He sang along, trying to put Lily out of his mind, concentrating on the road ahead.

At Tucson he turned directly south, on Highway 89, and headed down toward Nogales. He played the tape again and again, numbing his mind with the music.

It was late afternoon when he reached the border. Long shadows lay across the sand, cast by the cactus. There were other kinds of cactuses as well, and he wondered if mescal was among them, the kind Garland said was used to make their favorite drink, tequila. The thought of Garland reminded him of Lily again and the heat she would be taking from her family about that time. He wondered what Viv would say to her and then cut off the thought in his mind. He had come south to lick his own wounds.

The Mexican border patrol boarded the bus and took a keen interest in Buck's stereo equipment. He promised the two officers that he wouldn't try to sell the speakers and video set-up in their country, and he gave each one a can of Coors to show his good-will. He gave them the tape cassette, too, explaining in his broken Spanish that it was his voice. When they didn't believe him, he played the cassette and sang along one more time. The Mexicans politely applauded and sent Buck on his way.

He drove the winding roads of the Sierra Madre Occidental, through towns he had never visited—Imuris, Magdalena, Santa Ana. When Buck had come to this part of the country before, he had flown into a little airport further south with Garland, and they had gone to an island near the town of Bahía Kino, on the coast. Garland had gotten drunk on tequila and threatened to kill a man in a cantina. Buck's intervention had probably saved both their lives.

Shortly before midnight he stopped to eat re-fried beans and drink a Carta Blanca in a truck stop outside of Hermosillo. Then he locked himself inside the bus and fell asleep.

In the four weeks that Lily had been away, her father had transformed the farm. The junk cars that had been standing in weeds behind the barn for years had all been hauled off, and a new white picket fence surrounded the small, well-watered yard. The corn that Garland planted at the beginning of the summer, before the tour began, had all been harvested. Now he was putting in oats, laying down long, neat furrows with his new John Deere. The tractor was the same shiny green as the day it had been bought in Austin and shipped out to the hill country. Garland sat atop it like a ship's captain, charting his own course across the dun-colored fields.

Lily watched him plow for half an hour, trying to work up enough nerve to approach him. She stood in the shadow of the big cottonwood, by the water tank, hoping he would see her and motion her over, giving her no choice but to go. If Garland saw her, he gave no indication. Lily felt tense and drawn. Word of what had happened in Phoenix had spread faster than she had anticipated. There didn't seem to be a person in the county, or in the

166

Austin music scene, who didn't know. Lily had found her mother supportive, if saddened: she seemed to think that Lily had lost some part of herself forever, which in a way was true. She had just put her arms around her daughter, and it had been all Lily could do to keep from breaking down and crying.

Everyone seemed to blame Buck more than they blamed Lily. It wasn't fair. She tried to explain that she had gone after him, but people didn't want to hear about it. They believed that Buck had made a final choice between the road and his family and that Lily just happened to be mixed up in that larger question. That didn't make Lily feel very good, but she could see some truth in the assertion.

Finally Lily left the shade of the cottonwood tree and walked along the fence line, toward her father. She crossed the field, the freshly plowed earth spilling over the tops of her shoes. She paused to remove them and then walked on barefoot, feeling the coolness of the dirt between her toes. It was something she had seldom done as a child, since her father had been a traveling man instead of a farmer and the fields had been rented out to others.

Garland saw her at last. He didn't wave or cut the tractor's speed. He looked back at the blades again and continued on until he had finished the row. Then he cut the engine, lifted the plow, and sat there waiting.

"Daddy," she said, walking up to the big knobbed tire. She put a hand on it, unable to look him in the eye.

"Where's yer boyfriend?" He sounded distant and bored.

"I don't know," she said. "Mexico, I guess."

"You proud of yerself, Lil?"

She looked at him then. There were a lot of things about her that Garland still didn't know. One of those things was that she didn't sleep with just any guitar picker or harmonica player who came along. Buck had been different, even if he was her father's best friend.

"What do you think?" she asked.

"At least you had the guts to come back." Garland's eyes always protruded when he was angry, making him look like a man who had just wakened up. Lily remembered that from childhood. He had never hurt her and was generally good-natured, but Lily knew he was capable of violence.

She felt herself growing angry. Viv had put most of the blame on Buck, and now Garland was downgrading him, too. Lily's brief experience on the road had suggested things to her about her father's life that she might never have known. For instance, she was sure he had not always resisted the advances of the women who clustered around the musicians, as available as cold beer.

"Where in Mexico?" Garland asked.

"Probably the same place you used to go when you were hiding out from mom."

She had made her point. Garland blinked, staring down at her, some memory briefly interrupting his rage. Then he started the tractor again.

"Come on up here," he said, motioning.

Lily hesitated. Garland reached down, and she took his hand and swung aboard. She sat close to him on the molded metal seat.

"Hold on."

He swung the tractor around and headed for the barn, along the edge of the field. The motor was very loud, and the tractor lurched through the ruts. Occasionally Garland let one of the tires mash the ends of the new furrows, the only indication that he was in a hurry.

"You got a car here?" he shouted.

"Yeah."

"You're gonna drive me to the airport." He had a funny, determined look on his face. Lily realized that he was terribly hurt by what she and Buck had done.

"I'm so sorry, daddy," she shouted back at him.

"Yeah, you two are about the sorriest damn pair I ever met."

20

He caught the mid-afternoon flight between Austin and El Paso. He wore his Stetson and his dress boots; it was the first time he had been off the farm in a month. He hadn't told Rosella where he was going, and she had had the good sense not to ask. Garland traveled with only a lightweight western-style jacket and a valise that was part of a three-piece matching set Rosella had given him years before for road trips. The valise was small enough to carry on board the plane with him, but he checked it through, anyway. Stuffed inside, between his underwear and a clean shirt, was a .38-caliber revolver with pearl grips. The gun was loaded.

In El Paso he had to wait for a late-night flight to Hermosillo. He had a few tequila Sunrises in the bar while he waited to board, talking to no one, his feelings on a low burn. He had not been drunk in a long time, and the thirst had come over him at the first taste of the strong, slightly oily liquor. He could go for months without drinking anything more than an occasional beer. Then he could start putting the hard stuff away like it was his vocation, drinking for days on end, until his money ran out or he had the good sense to collapse. Usually the money ran out.

He boarded the little Mexican airliner just

before midnight. There were a few American tourists aboard, and some Latino businessmen, and Garland fell asleep listening to their chatter. He woke up several times, disturbed by troubled dreams he could not remember and the wilder air currents over northern Sonora state that buffeted the low-flying craft. Each time he thought about Lily and Buck. She was a woman now, and responsible for her own actions, but she was still his daughter. Buck should not have given in to her charms. He had violated Garland's trust, the strongest bond that existed between men, and Buck would have to answer for it.

The last time he woke up, the plane was on the ground at Hermosillo. It was still dark. He stumbled off in the wake of the tourists and claimed his bag. A single customs agent serviced the little airport, and Garland approached him confidently. He knew the official wouldn't search his bag or those of the tourists: they all looked respectable. Only the people who looked like desperadoes or hop heads got searched in Hermosillo—people who looked like Buck. Garland laughed, in spite of himself, at the memory of their previous visit, when Buck's baggage had been taken apart. A man with pigtails could have a hard time of it in Mexico.

The customs agent waved him through. A young woman in an official uniform smiled at Garland and asked in English if she could help him.

"Where can I get a taxi cab?" he asked.

"Where would you like to go, señor?"

"Bahía Kino."

The young woman raised her eyebrows. "That's an expensive cab fare, señor."

"Just point me to a cab," he told her. "And where can I get some whiskey?"

171

Buck woke up at first light. The screens on the windows of the old fishing shack he had rented were torn, but that didn't hurt the view any. He could see the putty-gray surface of the Gulf of California and a skiff with a tall, tattered sail moving slowly up-wind, toward the top of Tiburón Island. Within hours the water would assume its deep blue color, and gulls would come riding in from Baja, fifty miles due west.

He put on his sweat clothes and his jogging shoes and went out onto the porch. It was the coolest time of day, but severe heat would come up with the sun, just below the eastern horizon. There were no other shacks and no people near him, just the waves and the breeze and the salt smell he remembered from his previous visit. Garland had showed him how to find the stretch of beach the first time, and Buck had always thought of Tiburón, offshore from Bahía Kino, as a place to recover. He liked the solitude, but it had healed nothing. He couldn't even begin to sort it all out in his mind.

He ran on the beach until he had worked up a sweat. Then he went back to the shack. The bus was parked out back, and Buck went in and brought out his golf bag. The sign above the windshield, once used to show the bus's destination, read: Somewhere. He had written the word in there as a private joke, but he didn't really think it was funny. He didn't feel like he was somewhere; he felt like he was nowhere.

He climbed up on top of a sand dune. He took out a club—a 1-wood—and a ball, and teed it up on a little mound of sand. He spread his feet and addressed the ball as he had hundreds of times in cow pastures all over Texas. He drew the club back and came through with a hard, fast swing. The club face struck the ball with a solid *crack*. The

172

tiny white dot rose up against the luminous sky, seemed to hold there for a moment, and fell far out among the waves. Buck didn't see a splash.

He teed up another ball. When he looked up again, the sun had peeped over the hills behind him, touching the water with gold. Dawn had always been a time of inspiration for him, but he felt none that day. He was as empty as the landscape.

A cloud of dust rose against the sun. As Buck watched, a car took shape, speeding down the dirt road, swerving among the dunes and the low scrub growth. It did not turn back toward the ferry landing but plowed straight ahead. He felt a vague sense of foreboding. The car was close enough for him to see that it was a cab, and there were no cabs on Tiburón or in Bahía Kino, which meant it came all the way from Hermosillo. A single passenger rode in the back, gripping the roof through the open window.

It was Garland.

The cab slid to a stop, the dust drifting out over the dune. The driver and Garland began to argue, their voices loud in the early morning. Garland climbed out, pulling his valise after him, and threw some bills through the window. The driver cursed him in Spanish and then spun the wheels of the cab in the sand, gunning the motor. The car fishtailed and headed back up the road toward the ferry landing.

Buck and Garland looked at one another; neither of them waved. Garland picked up his bag and began to climb the dune.

Buck went back to his golf. He shuffled his feet and adjusted his grip, keeping his eye on the ball. He drew back slowly and drove it far out into the Gulf of California.

"Buck," said Garland. He was panting as he set the valise between his feet.

"Mornin', Garland." He reached into the golf bag for another old Top-Flight. "What do you want?"

Garland didn't answer. He opened his bag, too, and delved inside. He brought out a bottle of tequila. It was Sauza, one of the best brands, not like the local rotgut.

"You didn't come the whole way down here just for a drink," Buck said.

Garland reared back on his heels and took in the view. He was in no hurry; he didn't have to be. It had taken a lot of determination to get him to come this far, this fast. Buck wasn't going to get rid of him easily.

Garland said, "Peaceful as ever down here, ain't it?"

"It was."

Garland jerked the top off the tequila bottle. He tilted it up and took a long drink. He wiped his mouth with the back of his hand and offered the bottle to Buck. Buck hesitated, then accepted. He took a drink, feeling the hot liquor course through his body. He couldn't refuse, not if Garland was drinking, because being stone sober would put Buck at a disadvantage.

He handed the bottle back across. Garland tipped it up, then offered it to Buck again.

"Take another," he said. "It'll help us to talk. In fact, keep it."

Garland squatted down beside his valise and began to rummage around inside. "I got one for me in here, too." He jerked his head in the direction of the fishing shack. "You got anything to eat in there?"

"It's no use, Gar." Buck dropped the golf club and turned to face his old friend. "I don't want to talk."

Garland stared up at him, his eyes bulging. Buck knew that sign well enough.

"I figured you might not want to talk," Garland said. "That's why I brought this."

He pulled the pistol, not another bottle of Sauza, out of the valise. He held it casually in his right hand, on its side, the blunt noses of the bullets showing in the cylinder, the muzzle pointed in Buck's direction. Garland looked at the gun as if it were a plaything. Buck felt a hollowness in the pit of his stomach.

"Remember that fella I almost killed in the cantina down here that night?"

Buck almost smiled at the memory. The argument had concerned, typically, a pretty woman. Garland had thought he was being cut out by another man, on a night when he had a big thirst.

Buck just nodded.

"I only had half a bottle that night," Garland went on, "and that was on a full stomach."

"You'd never use that on me." Buck wanted to believe that.

"Not sober I wouldn't." Garland looked him over. Buck was the man who had slept with his daughter. "But when I git to the bottom of this bottle, I might." He produced another quart of Sauza.

"Yeah?" Buck said, half challenging him. "Well, when I get to the bottom of this one, I just might let you."

Buck took another swallow from the bottle, closing his eyes to the glare of the risen sun. There was, he decided, no point in dying sober.

Garland opened the new bottle and drank from it. He held the tequila in one hand and the pistol in the other.

"You silly old bastard," Buck said. The liquor was already taking effect.

"Now I'd say that's a good place to start the conversation, all right. 'Cause that's a pretty good title for you these last few weeks."

Buck could see that they were in for a long session. He left the golf clubs lying in the sand, walked around Garland, and started down the dune toward the shack. They might as well get something to eat, he thought, while they still had the chance.

Garland followed him, the valise in his arms, hampered by his bottle and the pistol.

"Don't blow yer foot off," Buck said over his shoulder. "It's a long enough walk home, as it is."

The waves had risen with the wind. They sat in wicker chairs on the porch, their feet propped on the railing, each nursing his own bottle. The sun was high now, and hot. Garland could feel the tequila oozing out through his pores, and the pleasant heightening of sensation brought on by the liquor. The light hovering about the fishing shack dazzled him. He had hoped the drinking would loosen Buck's tongue and get him to explain and express regret, but Buck seemed lost in his own problems.

The longer Garland waited for him to speak, the more he drank. And the more he drank, the angrier he became.

He held the bottle up against the blue sky; it was nearly empty.

"Look," he demanded, "I'm almost there." He put his hand threateningly on the pistol in his lap, but Buck didn't seem to notice.

Finally he said, "I didn't mean for it to happen, Garland."

Garland wanted to believe. At one point he thought Buck had taken advantage of Lily to get

176

back at him for quitting the band. But Buck wasn't like that. Garland blamed the traveling.

"It broke my heart when I heard, Buck. I swear, I wanted to tear you apart." He took a swig of tequila to cover the emotion that swept over him. He felt tears welling in his eyes.

Buck turned to him. "Garland—"

"You don't need to explain, I been on the road. I know how it goes."

"It wasn't that kinda thing at all," Buck said.

Garland lurched forward in his chair, grabbing up the pistol. The thought that his daughter might have been treated like some groupie drove him wild.

"Well, by God"—he brandished the .38—"you tell me what kinda thing it was, then!"

He stuck the barrel in Buck's face and pulled the hammer back. Garland wanted to see some remorse, and he wanted to see it fast. He realized that he was drunker than he had thought.

Buck grabbed the pistol and pushed it away. "I'm not asking you to forgive me," he said. "I just want you to understand it for what it was. Now let go of this silly pistol before somebody gets hurt."

"No, God damn it, you let go!"

They struggled over the gun.

"Put it down, Garland."

Enraged, Garland yanked on the handle. Buck held on. An explosion ripped through the air, the gun kicking free of both their hands. Buck screamed and fell backward, taking the chair over with him. Garland was barely aware of the sounds of breaking glass and the shrieks of gulls rising from the beach. "Oh, my God!"

He stumbled forward and went down on his knees, horrified. "Buck, you all right?"

His eyes were open, at least. He lay flat on his

back, his hand on his side. Slowly he raised himself on one elbow. Garland thought he could be dying, he was so pale and shaky. They both watched as Buck gathered his strength and slipped his hand away from his side.

The shirt was torn, but there was no blood on the material. The bullet had missed him.

Buck stuck his finger into the hole. "Jesus, man!" he shouted. "I hope you're happy! You ruined my damn shirt!"

Garland fell back against the railing. The anger and resentment drained out of him, replaced by sheer relief that Buck was not wounded. He felt around on the floor for his bottle. Buck's bottle had been broken in the fall, but Garland still had tequila left. He took a swallow and handed the bottle to Buck. The liquor no longer had any effect; Garland was stone sober.

"I damn near killed you," he said.

"Yeah, you damn near did." Buck thought about it for a moment and began to laugh. He tossed the empty bottle away.

"It ain't funny, Buck."

Garland struggled to his feet. He offered his hand to Buck, who hesitated, and then took it, letting Garland pull him up. They regarded one another sheepishly. This time they laughed together and spontaneously embraced. Buck slapped him on the back.

"I think I'm gonna need me some more tequila," Garland said.

"Yeah, me, too. There's that little cantina down the beach. Then let's get off this island."

The bus sat alone on the ferry deck, jostled by the waves. The old diesel engine sputtered and coughed, and Buck wondered if they would make it to the mainland. He didn't really care one way or the other. He didn't know where he was going after the ferry docked; he just had to get away from the place where he had narrowly missed being killed.

He and Garland leaned on the stern railing, without speaking, watching Tiburón recede in the distance. They had armed themselves with fresh bottles of tequila. Buck considered his own state of inebriation as the only rational way to deal with the loss of his girl, his wife, and his friends. He assumed Garland was in a similar condition.

Garland took the pistol out of his pocket, and they studied it together. It was an old gun, and well-traveled. Garland had often carried it for what he termed self-protection, although often as not it was the other person who needed protecting.

"Why was it I wanted to kill that fella in the cantina that time?" Garland asked. "I can't even remember."

"You said he stole your gal from you."

Garland smiled. "Well, he did try to walk out with her."

"As I recall," Buck said, "she was the man's wife." He didn't have to point out that anybody could act like a fool over a woman, given the right provocation.

"No, she wasn't." Garland seemed genuinely astonished. "Was she?"

Buck nodded.

Garland dropped the pistol into the swirling wake of the ferry. The trailing gulls swooped down, thinking it was food, then rose again into the air, squawking in disappointment. Neither of them spoke for a while, lulled by the engine's vibration and the effects of the sun and the tequila. Finally Buck couldn't hold the question any longer.

"How is she, Garland?" he asked softly.

Garland looked at him but didn't answer. Buck knew his own pain was obvious to his old friend, but maybe not the identity of the woman in question. Buck had been speaking of Viv, not Lily.

He took another drink.

21

Lily drove out from Austin to the Bonham ranch. She had put the visit off as long as possible. It had been easier for her to confront her father, with his rage and his deep disappointment, than to face up to Viv Bonham. Viv was as strong as any man Lily knew, Garland Ramsey included, and she had also been a friend. Lily had always admired the way Viv stayed home to look after Jamie. Lily thought it was wrong of her to pressure Buck to retire—he was too important to stop playing—but Lily sympathized with anyone who had been left behind. She was sure Viv blamed her some for her own betrayal, and for Buck's as well.

She turned in at the mailbox marked Honeysuckle Rose. She followed the winding dirt road along the creek and over the dilapidated old bridge. Viv's car was parked in the shade of the cottonwoods; there was no sign of Jamie. Lily hoped he was off somewhere riding his pony. She couldn't bear facing both of them.

Lily pulled up beside the front gate and stepped out into the grass. The Bonham place was more beautiful than her own, with the pond and the nestling hills around. It was also less well-kept, but it had more of a feeling of tradition about it. The Bonhams had been on the land longer than the

Ramseys. The fields had never been used for anything but pasture.

She crossed the yard and climbed the steps to the porch. She knocked on the screen door and waited, sticking her hands down into the pockets of her Levis to cover her nervousness. But no one came to receive her. She considered walking back to her car, quickly getting in, and returning to Austin. But then she would just have to come out another time; her conscience wouldn't let her stay away.

She opened the screen door and stepped inside, just as she had done dozens of times when she had come to give guitar lessons to Jamie.

She called tentatively, "Viv?"

There was no answer. She was about to call again, when Jamie came into the hall. He wore his boots and his cowboy hat, but he wasn't swaggering the way he thought cowboys had to. Instead, he stared at Lily with very wide eyes.

"Jamie."

He didn't return her greeting, and she knew then that he knew. The thought made her sadder than ever.

"Is your mother home?"

He called out to Viv. She appeared, behind him, and put her hands on his shoulders. She didn't speak to Lily, either. Her hair was tied up in a bandanna, and she wore a denim shirt with the top snap undone. She looked good, Lily thought.

"It's Lily, mom," Jamie said, as if his mother might have forgotten. Lily realized how surprised he was to see her.

"I don't think we have anything to say to each other," Viv told her.

"No, please let me talk." It was important to her. "Just for a minute."

"Okay, go ahead."

"Can we be alone?" Lily asked. Lily had a vague notion that they could work everything out, woman to woman.

"Jamie's as much involved in this as I am," Viv said.

The explanations and the appeals that Lily had constructed in her mind evaporated under Viv's and Jamie's collective gaze.

"It's very hard," Lily admitted.

"Yeah, I know."

"I know it sounds impossible, but I love you and Jamie."

Viv didn't respond. She was giving no quarter.

"What can I do?" Lily asked.

Viv still didn't answer. She just turned her head and stared out the front window, toward the pasture. Lily felt like asking Viv if she had never had an affair. She was independent, too. At least Lily knew how to admit that she had been wrong.

"Viv, I've come to apologize."

"Thank you."

It was the best Lily could do. Without another word, she turned and left the house.

Final preparations were underway for the Labor Day concert. Viv took Jamie with her and drove over to the site. The lights were being rigged on the towers, with men climbing up and down the scaffolding like insects. Huge speakers were being lifted by crane up onto the wings of the stage, where workers stood holding squawking radios, talking back and forth between one another and the operators of the big machinery. The whole project had taken on a life of its own as the men rushed to get ready for the crowds the next day. Electricians drove up and down in four-wheel-drive vehicles between the stage and the huge junction box at the top of the hill. Cases of beer and soft drinks were being unloaded from trucks lined up at the concession stands. Five men were unrolling security fencing and attaching it to tall metal poles that had been set in concrete.

Jamie took it all in, tightly clutching Viv's hand. Finally he said, with awe in his voice, "This was just an empty field, mom."

She tried to match his excitement, but she felt none herself. Buck had not come home, and now Garland was gone. That meant she and the band would have to carry the burden of the concert themselves. Viv didn't look forward to that.

"It'll all be full of people tomorrow," she told Jamie.

"Goddam daddy," he said. "Why's he want to spoil something terrific as this?"

"Watch your language, Jamie."

The speakers were hooked up, and a man announced a sound check, his voice booming out over the land.

"Testing—one—two—three—testing. Mary had a little lamb, she tied him to a heater. And every time he turned around, he burned his little peter. . . ."

Jamie looked up at her and raised his hands in a gesture of confusion. Viv wanted to laugh, he looked so disgusted with adults.

"Viv!"

She turned around and saw Rosella standing beside one of the concession stands, supervising the unloading. She waved, and Viv waved, and they ran toward one another.

Garland woke up to see the bus plowing along the shoulder of the highway. Buck was at the wheel, obviously drunk. He jerked the bus back onto the pavement, but it went all the way across and began to plow along the shoulder on the other side. Luckily, there were no cars in sight. Dust rose up in clouds behind them. Ahead, the sky looked bruised at the onset of another long Mexican night.

Buck got the wheels onto the highway, but they seemed to weave with a life of their own. He cursed good-naturedly.

"Damn road won't hold still."

Garland let out a rodeo yell. He wasn't as drunk as Buck, but he was far from sober.

"How did we get on this bus?" Buck wanted to know.

"Wasn't nothin' to it." He had tricked Buck into taking a little ride after they got back to the mainland. Buck had passed out, and Garland had driven through most of the Sierra Madre range listening to him talk in his sleep about Lily, and Viv. At least it had kept Garland awake.

"Weren't we in a cantina?" Buck said.

"That was two days ago—or hours."

They both got a good laugh out of that one. The bus swerved violently to the left. Garland looked out in time to see a peasant steering his burro cart into the ditch. The peasant dove into a patch of cane.

"I think you better let me drive," he said.

"I'm doin' fine."

This time Garland looked up and saw a roadside sign disappear beneath the bus. He heard it bang the length of the chassis, before they left it in the dirt.

"You're drunk," Garland said. "Lemme drive."

Buck was insulted. "I ain't drunk, Garland!"

If Buck wasn't drunk, Garland thought, then something was wrong with him. He had started drinking tequila again as soon as he had wakened, and that had been hours before.

"I know you drunk," Garland told him, "and I

185

know you sober. You're drunk. Now, dammit, Buck, lemme drive!"

Buck was outraged. He glared at Garland, then stood up and just walked away from the wheel.

"Well, hell, go on and take it, then."

The bus started to wobble. Their luggage tumbled from the overhead rack. The bottle of Sauza that Buck had set down beside him turned over and began to drain onto the floorboards.

Garland leaped for the wheel and brought the bus under control. Now he was definitely sober.

"I wish you wouldn't do that kind'a shit, Buck."

Buck retrieved his bottle and fell back in the shotgun seat. He laughed at Garland's concern and took another drink.

"Which way we headed, anyway?"

Garland wasn't sure he was ready to hear the truth. But he said casually, "That sign you bulldozed said Texas."

"Texas! I ain't goin' back to Texas!" He staggered to his feet. "Turn this sonofabitch around!"

Garland hit the brakes. He put the bus into a skid, on purpose, and jerked on the wheel, throwing Buck to the floor. He backed up onto the shoulder and turned the bus in a complete circle. Buck rolled out into the aisle.

"Garland, you silly bastard!"

"Well, you said you didn't wanna go back to Texas." He was counting on Buck not knowing what direction he was traveling in.

Buck pulled himself back up into the seat. It was almost dark now; he barely glanced out the window.

"I can't go back, anyway," he said, with a touch of sadness.

"It'd be awful hard, all right."

"At least this way nobody's tryin' to nail my damn feet to the floor."

Garland pretended to be in sympathy with him. "The road's wide open for you now, Buck."

"Yeah." Buck sighed, gazing out at the empty landscape bathed in shadow. "Now I can search out some new folks to sing them old songs to."

"Yeah."

They rode in silence for several miles.

"Too bad," Garland said, "that you can't come up with some *new* songs to sing to them *old* friends." He gave his companion, and old friend, a long look. "Don't you get tired, Buck?"

That got to him, Garland could tell. Buck shifted uneasily.

"Lately," he admitted, "it ain't been no day at the beach, Gar."

It was completely dark. A pair of headlights appeared on the horizon, or was it stars? The land had flattened out again, as monotonous as west Texas.

"You miss the road, Garland?"

He had expected that question for days. Buck was bound to want to know how it felt to finally quit, but his pride hadn't let him ask it until now.

"Well, I tell you," Garland said, putting off the answer, "I bought me a John Deere tractor and planted eighty acres of oats. Now I'm out there in the field every day watching clouds, worryin' whether or not it's gonna rain. In between time, I'm readin' up on bugs. There's more varieties of them little bastards gonna try to eat my oats than you can shake a stick at—speckled bugs, polka-dotted bugs, green bugs. I'm tryin', but goddamn, it's hard for me to build up enough animosity to wanna kill one of them little shit-asses. . . ."

Garland trailed off. He hadn't answered Buck's question, at least not with words.

Buck said, "You miss it that much, huh?"

"After thirty years of it, yeah," he admitted. "Goddamnit, I do miss it."

"You got a woman who loves you, though."

"That's true," Garland said. "And I love her. We struggled, but by God, it was worth it. We love each other more than ever now."

Buck took a quick pull on the tequila bottle. He sounded angry when he spoke. "I just ain't ready to give it up yet, that's all."

"Viv knows that," he said. "She just wanted to be part of your life, Buck. She never asked for the whole thing, did she?"

Buck thought about it. "No, she never did ask for the whole thing. I guess I wasn't listening."

The lights had turned out to be stars, after all. Gradually more appeared in the sky. The breeze coming in the side window had grown a little cooler. It was going to be a nice night, Garland thought, for making good time on the road.

"You love her, Buck?"

"That's the hell of it," he said. "I do love her."

Garland smiled inwardly. Buck sounded a lot less drunk.

"I tell you," Buck went on, "when Viv came walkin' out there on that stage, I knew in that instant where the best part of my life really was—and how I'd just lost it."

Garland scoffed at him. "I never seen you lose anything you didn't wanna lose."

"I don't know how to go back, Garland. Not after all this."

"You said you love her," Garland reminded him.

Buck stared straight ahead, thinking. Then he took a deep, determined breath.

"Turn this sonofabitch around," he said.

Garland threw his head back and laughed. Then he stomped on the accelerator.

"Garland, you hear me? I said—"

"We're goin' right," Garland told him triumphantly. "Texas is this-aways."

"I thought you said—" Buck looked behind the bus. He thought Garland had turned around, miles back.

"Well," Garland said, "I guess I had so much faith in you I just lied."

They both laughed. Garland smacked the wheel with his open palm and let out a heart-felt rodeo whoop.

"Hang on," he said. "I'm gonna give this ole mule a kick."

The bus began to pick up speed.

22

All morning Viv expected the telephone to ring. It was just a feeling she had, a kind of premonition that Buck would call or show up at the last minute before the concert began. It was too late to cancel the show, and it wasn't fair to the people who were already traveling from miles away to hear Buck play with the band. Viv and the others could try to carry the performance without him, but Buck's fans would be disappointed. Some of them might even get mad and misbehave.

Viv told herself that her concerns were only with business, but deep down she didn't really care about the fans. They would survive. It was Buck she worried about. She had been more angry than hurt the night she saw him on the stage with Lily in St. Louis. Buck had always appeared in different lights to Viv; it was one of the pleasures of living with him. He could seem as handsome and impassive as a chiseled stone monument or impish or infinitely wise. But that night he had reminded her of an old goat without the good sense to leave temptation alone. Viv had never been much good at controlling her wrath, and she had a mean tongue when she wanted to use it. She had honed it while on the road herself, dealing with male hecklers. She tended to go straight to the problem, and that night the problem had been right on stage. Now she wondered if it had been a good idea to embarrass Buck in front of his friends and the audience. They had all come back to Austin without him, including Lily. Viv knew that wherever Buck was, he was suffering.

She almost felt sorry for him. The night before, she had been unable to sleep for worrying about him. Jamie must have had the same problem, for he crawled into bed with her around midnight. He understood what had happened between Lily and his father. Jamie was remarkably accepting of Buck's unpredictability and his long absences. What he couldn't accept was the idea of a future without Buck. But he was afraid to ask about that, and Viv was afraid to think about it.

By noon there had been no word from Buck, and Viv knew he wouldn't telephone, after all. She put her guitar in the back seat, and she and Jamie drove over the hills to the concert. Buck Bonham's Band was due to play in an hour. A thousand cars were parked in the pasture adjacent to the fence. A long line stretched back from the gate. Those people with tickets flooded through, carrying blankets and coolers. Others crowded around the concession stands, buying armloads of Pearl and Lone Star, or lay on the grass eating picnic lunches, drinking, smoking. They applauded the local Austin group on the stage, in the warm-up spot, picking and singing for all they were worth. But it was Buck and the boys that the people were waiting for.

Viv drove down to the bottom of the pasture, and a security guard let her through the gate. She and Jamie climbed the stairs to the wings. The big speakers throbbed with the sound of country music. The new group was good, Viv thought professionally, but they lacked punch. She realized that she was nervous without Buck there to sing with her, and a little lost. But she had organized the event, and it was up to her to bring it off.

The others were waiting. Rosella hurried over and gave Viv a hug, her glistening eyes proof that Garland had not come home, either. He and Buck were either drunk somewhere together or dead. Neither prospect gave the women much comfort.

Bonnie smiled warmly at her, and the rest of the band members said hello. But the old joshing was missing. They were all wishing they could be someplace else, and Viv didn't blame them.

She took her guitar out of the case and began to tune it. To cover her nervousness, she played a few chords, but she was rusty. Each time she made a mistake, Jamie winced.

Sid came backstage wearing a new wide-brimmed hat with a rattlesnake-skin band. He seemed nervous, too.

"This is their last song, kids," he announced. "Ready, Viv?"

She nodded and messed up another chord.

Jamie said, "Maybe you ought'a just sing, mom."

The group on stage played the chorus of "Honky Tonk Heroes," and the music trailed off. They were applauded as they made their exit, bowing and waving their hats. Viv's nervousness turned to something close to terror. She gained new respect for Buck's ability and ease when he was alone on stage before a big crowd.

She led the others out. The sun shone brightly on thousands of upturned faces, on the colorful array of blankets spread on the grass, on bright clothes and bare chests, and on the distant sea of parked cars. The applause grew louder, mixed with shouts and whistles as the audience recognized the members of Buck Bonham's Band. Viv was grateful for the reception. She hugged the guitar and leaned to the mike.

"Thank you," she said, her voice echoing out over the land. "As you know, this whole affair is being thrown in honor of a dear friend of ours, and of many of you—Garland Ramsey."

The name brought another wave of clapping. Viv waited for it to subside and then told them, "Garland isn't here right now. Also, as many of you already know if you've been listening to our apologies on the radio, my husband isn't going to be here, either." She paused again. The audience was quiet now, but Viv was afraid she would choke up.

"I'm sorry," she said, "but if anyone wants his money back—"

Kelly stepped forward and touched her arm. "Just sing, Viv. We don't need nobody else."

The microphone picked up his voice, and the crowd applauded that, too.

They began to play.

The sign read Austin—10 Miles. Garland passed it traveling seventy miles an hour, the old bus shaking like a dying man. It might never recover from the trip, he thought, wheeling off the Interstate and into a diesel lane at the truck stop. Buck lay limply in the seat beside him, snoring, holding a half-filled bottle of tequila in his lap.

Garland opened the window and told the attendant, "Fill 'r up." Then he took the bottle from Buck's hands and shoved it under the front seat. He shook his friend awake.

"Let's get some coffee, Buck."

Buck opened his eyes, unaware of how close he was to home. Garland was determined to get them both to the concert, drunk or sober. He had never been quite as tired as he was at that moment, but they had only a few miles to go. He wasn't giving up now.

They stumbled off the bus and went into the restaurant. Coffee cups were lined up on the counter in front of the stools, and the waitress stood ready with a glass coffee pot. The sight of Buck didn't please her, with his braided hair, dirty clothes, bleary eyes, and the way he slumped forward onto her counter. Garland didn't look much better. He caught a glimpse of himself in the mirror, and tried to stuff his shirttail back into his trousers before she noticed. His hair hung down in his eyes, and he let out an involuntary groan as he sank onto the stool.

The waitress said to Garland, "Coffee, honey?"

He nodded and jerked his thumb at Buck. "Fill 'r up. The oil and water's okay."

They both thought that was very funny, but the waitress didn't seem to get the joke. She looked hard and long at Buck as she filled his cup.

"You're Buck Bonham, ain't you?"

"I used to be," Buck told her.

"I hope neither of you is driving."

This time it wasn't the waitress talking. Garland looked along the counter and felt his breath drain away. Two highway patrolmen sat watching them, their heads bent forward, their sunglasses in place. The one closest to Garland had his hand resting on his hip, inches from the handle of a revolver in a tooled leather holster. Neither cop was smiling.

Buck had seen them, too. He and Garland exchanged glances. Then they pointed at one another and said at the same time, "He is!"

She sang without the guitar, the words coming from deep inside her, the stage fright forgotten. She stepped back from the mike to let the band play the musical break. They seemed moved by the intensity of Viv's emotion. She knew that she was singing for Buck and for herself and that the music was the only way of expressing the contradictory love she felt.

I'll tell all about how you cheated.
I'd like for the whole world to know.
I'd like to get even with you for your leavin',
But sad songs and waltzes
Aren't selling this year.

She sought out Jamie among the crowd of people standing in the wings. He stood behind the huge bank of speakers, watching, Rosella's arm around his shoulders. Viv knew he was having as much trouble as she keeping the tears down.

The bus careened along the narrow country road. Buck and Garland sat side-by-side in the shotgun seat, watching the highway patrolman handle the wheel like a real professional. His sleeves were rolled up, and he pressed the accelerator to the floor in an attempt to keep up with his partner in the squad car up ahead. The siren cut through the afternoon calm, and the red light inside the bubble-gum machine dome on top of the car revolved wildly. The cops had decided that it was worth getting Buck and Garland to the concert alive.

The bus topped the hill, and Buck could see the crowd massed in the little valley. The cop in the squad car cut the siren as they raced along the fence, past the main gate, and down the hill toward the rear of the stage. He thought he heard the sound of Viv's voice and the distinct rhythm produced by his band when they were playing in top form.

He pushed his face out the open window, into

195

the warm, rushing air of early September, to confirm it. Viv's voice soared from the speakers. For a moment Buck forgot that he had come back to make amends and perform if she and the band, and the audience, still wanted him. He just wanted to listen to his wife sing.

The security guards let the squad car and bus in through the rear gate. They pulled to a halt in a cloud of dust, and he and Garland piled off. Buck shook the driver's hand and that of his partner. His head ached, and he felt shaky from the days of drinking and smoking, but nothing could have kept him away from that stage.

As he heard Viv sing the reprise of her song, Buck turned around and saw many of his friends standing on the rear of the stage and in the grass, beaming at him. Garland and Rosella were in one another's arms. Buck was looking for one face in particular, and finally he found it. Jamie stood alone on the stairs, watching him intently, waiting for some sign.

Buck grinned. Jamie ran forward, his arms outstretched, and Buck swept him off the ground and held him tightly. He kissed him and whispered, "Come on, kid. I'm gonna need yer help in this one."

He set him on the ground, and Jamie took his hand. Together they walked up the stairs. The band had finished the number, and the applause rolled out over the hills. They paused in the wings, watching while Viv acknowledged the fans' appreciation. Buck thought she looked beautiful in her denim shirt and jeans, but sad, too.

The clapping began to subside, and Buck and Jamie walked out onto the boards. Viv had her back to them. The applause rose again as the audience recognized Buck Bonham. He was going to surprise Viv on stage as she had surprised him, but with a different intention and, he hoped, a different effect.

Viv was glancing from one side to the other, trying to figure out who the audience was applauding. Buck and Jamie walked right up behind her, and Buck put a hand gently on her shoulder. She turned, her face registering surprise, and then a kind of dismay. Buck realized that she didn't know exactly how to react, that she was torn between love and a lingering resentment. He didn't blame her. She didn't avert her eyes. For a long moment they stared at one another, the audience growing quiet in bewilderment and anticipation.

Finally Buck said, "I'm sorry, Viv."

Her face softened, but she didn't respond. It was still up to Buck to carry the show.

"Let me prove it," he added.

Slowly she recovered from the shock of discovering him on the stage with her. She turned and pulled the microphone to her and announced, "Ladies and gentlemen, Buck Bonham."

The crowd went wild.

"Come on, Jamie," Viv said, taking his hand and walking toward the wings without another glance at Buck.

He picked up her guitar and passed the strap over his head. He didn't know what the verdict was, whether she would forgive him or not, but he would do everything he could to make her forgive him. If he had ever put his heart into a song, he would do it now. He had thought up some crazy words that morning at dawn, in case they made it to Austin in time. His words and his talent were all Buck had to offer.

Garland joined him on the stage, carrying his own guitar. Buck acknowledged him and the other grinning band members. They were all waiting.

197

"Go ahead, Buck," Garland urged.

He hit the strings, put his head back, and began.

There was no sound from the audience. As Buck sang, he let his gaze swing over the crowd, the fence, and the parking lot, to the hills and sky beyond. It was his country, he was home. The road led from home to a thousand different places, and although he felt the pull of the road still, he knew he would eventually end up where he stood, in the county of his ancestors and of his child.

Buck searched out Viv and Jamie in the wings. They stood watching him, Jamie's hand in hers.

ABOUT THE AUTHOR

ROBERT ALLEN is the author of *Shampoo, Last Tango in Paris* and *The Front*.

RELAX!
SIT DOWN
and Catch Up On Your Reading!

THE LATEST BOOKS
IN THE BANTAM
BESTSELLING TRADITION

Bantam Book Catalog

Here's your up-to-the-minute listing of over 1,400 titles by your favorite authors.

This illustrated, large format catalog gives a description of each title. For your convenience, it is divided into categories in fiction and non-fiction—gothics, science fiction, westerns, mysteries, cookbooks, mysticism and occult, biographies, history, family living, health, psychology, art.

So don't delay—take advantage of this special opportunity to increase your reading pleasure.

Just send us your name and address and 50¢ (to help defray postage and handling costs).